LORRAINE WILSON

I live in Wiltshire with my husband but love to travel and have lived in four continents. From playing amidst Roman ruins in Africa as a child to riding a Sultan's racehorse in the Middle East as a teen, I've many experiences to draw on for the stories I've been writing ever since I can remember. When I'm not writing you'll find me listening to audiobooks while I sew or design handbags, usually with a rescue terrier or two curled up on my feet!

Secret Crush of a Chalet Girl

LORRAINE WILSON

Harper*Impulse* an imprint of
HarperCollins*Publishers Ltd*
77–85 Fulham Palace Road
Hammersmith, London W6 8JB

www.harpercollins.co.uk

A Paperback Original 2014

First published in Great Britain in ebook format by Harper*Impulse* 2014

A catalogue record for this book
is available from the British Library

ISBN: 978-0-00-759173-2

This novel is entirely a work of fiction.
The names, characters and incidents portrayed in it are
the work of the author's imagination. Any resemblance to
actual persons, living or dead, events or localities is
entirely coincidental.

Automatically produced by Atomik ePublisher from Easypress

*Thanks as always to the lovely team at Harper
Impulse and also to my husband for believing that
cocktail tasting at very nice hotels was essential for
the writing of this book!*

CHAPTER ONE

"So, what's that you're reading?"

Tash's voice pierced Sophie's happy bubble like a razor slashing a party balloon.

"Just a book." Sophie shifted on her bar stool, inching the Kindle screen away from Tash's line of sight.

Tash slid onto the cow-skin bar stool next to her and didn't seem to pick up on Sophie's irritation at being disturbed.

"You're early." Tash swiveled towards her. "We're not meeting until eight."

"I wanted a bit of time alone," Sophie replied.

Fat chance of that around here, or in the dorm room at Chalet Repos, or…anywhere for that matter.

Privacy was the only luxury in short supply in Verbier.

"Me too, those kids were making a right racket back at the chalet. I wish Scott would make it an adults-only chalet." Tash grimaced.

Sophie sighed heavily. Time to relinquish her vain hope for a bit of peace and quiet. There was no stopping Tash if she'd decided she wanted to talk to you. Things were certainly…difficult back at Chalet Repos, for more than one reason. But it wasn't anything she wanted to talk to Tash about.

"So, what are you reading Ms. Trent? Why don't you want to tell me?" Tash had grabbed Sophie's Kindle before Sophie could stop her.

Sophie glared at Tash, who scrolled through the pages on-screen, a delighted smile on her face.

"Ooh, it's a romance. I didn't know you were into these bodice-rippers." Tash's cat-like eyes gleamed, reflecting the bar's tea lights. "So, what page are the dirty bits on?"

"Ssh, will you keep it down?" Sophie reached for the Kindle but Tash lifted it above her head. She was only attracting more attention now from the other customers of Bar des Amis, some of them starting the après ski early, while others clearly hadn't made it back to their accommodation to change from their ski gear yet. A hot flush crept up Sophie's neck and heat radiated from her cheeks.

She automatically cast her eyes down to the floor – the way she'd always coped whenever she wanted to disappear.

What she'd give for a trap door right now. Or even just a chance to escape into her book again.

"Nathan tenderly stroked the side of Ava's face. Yet despite the tenderness, his dark eyes blazed with the heat of passion and her skin tingled at his touch. 'Do you feel it too?' he asked huskily as their eyes locked," Tash read aloud in a ridiculously over-the-top acting voice. "Then he reached for her, his mouth was on her lips, tasting her hungrily as his hands slid down to cup her…"

"For God's sake, Tash, will you just shut up?" Sophie spoke fiercely into Tash's ear, fighting the feelings of humiliation. She knew Tash wasn't deliberately trying to ridicule her but this felt too much like all those horrible times at school for comfort. It felt like Tash had ripped all of Sophie's clothes off, leaving her exposed for everyone to laugh at her, plump and naked except for her mis-matched underwear.

At last Sophie managed to grab the Kindle back and slumped, mortified, onto her bar stool.

"Ça va?"

Sophie looked up to see who had spoken, afraid she'd find the owner of the voice laughing at her. Instead she found the dark-grey eyes of Luc Dubois, the owner of Bar des Amis, fixed on her.

The very gorgeous bar owner.

Who'd just heard everything Tash had said. Not that she was ashamed of liking romance novels but it was private, something she kept to herself precisely to stop things like this occurring. And it was too precious an escape for it to be exposed to ridicule. Books had always been her escape – in the school library, where she'd hid from the bullies at lunchtime, devouring the Sweet Valley High series and then here in Verbier. When it seemed everyone was finding love except for her the romance novels on her Kindle had provided solace. Given her hope.

She shrugged, fighting the lie rising to her lips, unwilling to automatically say the 'Oui, bien merci', socially accepted response. For one thing it felt like Luc actually wanted to know, rather than just a standard greeting.

His grey eyes flickered with sympathy. Sophie couldn't imagine he knew what it felt like to be ridiculed or bullied. Luc was cool without trying. His dark hair looked wilder than ever this evening, as though he'd just rolled out of bed and sloped down to open up the bar, his handsome jaw peppered with stubble. Maybe he had. For a second she wondered who he'd been in bed with. He was gorgeous enough to have his pick of the Verbier lovelies.

Don't be ridiculous Sophie, as if someone like him would be interested in you.

She chided herself. He was out of her league, so what was the point of speculating? She might be average size back in the UK but here she was slightly plump, the only bonus being large, real, breasts. Also she was very definitely not cool without trying. In fact she had to try very hard just to fit in. She spent more than she should getting her hair coloured and highlighted to a perfect caramel blonde before she came out for the Verbier season each year, blowing all the tips she made in the summer at Uncle Frank's café.

As it was she fitted in but she would never stand out. A 'six out of ten' she'd heard a group of guys rating her the other night. So while she'd love the intent look Luc was giving her to mean more, he was just being kind.

Luc jerked his head towards Tash, who was now having a noisy conversation with one of the instructors from the Swiss Ski School. "Ignore her, Sophie. It's not important."

He knows who I am.

She loved how he said her name, his Swiss-French accent making it sound special, as though it weren't entirely ordinary. Just like her.

"It's important to me," she replied quietly. The days of being bullied at school might be in the past, dead and buried, but she couldn't deny the ghosts still had the power to kick her where it hurt.

She felt the flush on her cheeks growing hotter for a reason entirely different than embarrassment and tried to ignore the sweet unfurling sensation in the pit of her stomach. Well it was actually a fair bit lower than her stomach…

He's too good-looking for you. Sixes don't go out with tens, not in the real world.

"Désolée. I'm sorry," Luc said softly. "But even so, don't let it get to you."

Easier said than done.

"You don't really believe that romance crap, do you?" Tash's voice gate-crashed the intimate moment between Sophie and Luc.

Normally Sophie liked Tash. They'd been friends and colleagues for a couple of seasons now but tonight Tash was really winding her up. At her best she was like an over-enthusiastic puppy – loyal and emotionally honest. At her worst she could teach a bull in a china shop a thing or two.

"Yes, I do," Sophie replied defiantly. "I believe there are men out there who can be romantic and that falling in love could happen to any one of us."

Tash snorted. "True love, the one, a magical connection? I just don't get it. And if buying a bunch of flowers when men have done something they feel guilty about is romantic, well, give me realism any day. It's all about sex, pure and simple."

"Just because you haven't fallen in love yet doesn't mean that you never will," Sophie said with conviction. "And you can laugh all you like but romance books are really popular, they sell well so I can't be the only one who likes them."

"Hi you two, what've we missed?" Amelia grabbed the free bar stool next to Sophie and Lucy moved in on the other side of Tash, waving at Luc to get his attention so she could order a drink.

Sophie seethed quietly. She might as well have stayed back at the chalet for all the peace and quiet she was getting here. Were Amelia and Lucy also fleeing the noise of the kids' bedtime routine back at Chalet Repos? She glared at Tash, willing her to drop the subject now the others were here.

"We've been reading from *Intimate Surrender*," Tash said, taking a sip from her cocktail, seemingly oblivious to the furious vibes Sophie sent in her direction. "Our Sophie is a bit of a romance fan on the quiet."

"Yeah, I can't think why I kept my reading tastes quiet." Sophie rolled her eyes. "Oh yes, that would be because I knew you'd make fun of me. Although I hadn't anticipated the whole public humiliation scenario. Thanks for that."

Luc caught Sophie's gaze and winked at her while he got the girls' drinks. She'd felt a delicious stirring of desire inside and tried to quash it.

He's just being nice, that's all.

"Those books are a bit unrealistic," Lucy said, now perched on a bar stool and sipping at the cocktail Luc had put in front of her. She was so petite she looked like a tiny, fierce bird but her no-nonsense, matter-of-fact manner made you underestimate her at your peril.

"But if you want real life you just have to open your eyes. Books are so much more than that, they take you into different worlds, they open up your mind." Sophie slipped her Kindle into her bag and firmly tugged the zip closed before Tash could think about taking it and reading aloud from it again. She didn't feel she'd made her case properly and it frustrated her.

"If they make you believe in Prince Charming, aren't you going to be disappointed when the belching Mr. Average leaves his socks on the bathroom floor?" Amelia asked.

Great, three against one.

"I'm not expecting Prince Charming," she faltered.

Just Mr.-Right-For-Me.

Tash snorted. "You could've fooled me. When was the last time you had sex? Who exactly are you holding out for? I hate to disappoint you but I think Prince Harry is taken; he looked pretty loved-up last time he was in Verbier."

Lucy choked on her drink, clearly still not used to Tash's forthrightness, even though they were nearly ten weeks into the season.

Sophie narrowed her eyes at Tash, refusing to answer, horribly aware of Luc, still in earshot. Not that he had any reason to be interested in their conversation, but…

"It's been a while, girl," Tash continued, in her usual blunt manner.

Sophie sighed. It was much easier to humour Tash than argue with her. And the quicker the better. It was the only way to shut her up.

"Okay, yes, it's been a while," she admitted quietly.

"We could go off to the Hotel Royale's hot tub if you're looking for some action," Tash suggested.

"I might as well hang a sign over my head saying I'm desperate. Which I'll have you know I'm not." Sophie's eyes flickered involuntarily over to Luc, but he stood with his back to them, taking a bottle down from the shelf, no indication he was listening.

And why would he be?

She wasn't interested in the kind of casual sex Tash was talking about. She'd been there and done that and had got a whole lot more than a T-shirt for her trouble.

Next time it needs to mean something. It has to…

"I'd be desperate if I hadn't had sex for a year," Amelia said, grinning.

"It's going well with Matt then, if that smile is anything to go by?" Tash asked.

"Great thanks, he's coming out for Valentine's Day, for the whole weekend in fact." The wattage of Amelia's smile increased until she was beaming.

"Aw, sweet," Tash replied.

Sophie thought she saw a flash of something like envy in Tash's cat-like eyes but it quickly disappeared to be replaced by a dark screen.

When Tash headed off for the loos Sophie followed her.

"Are you okay?" Sophie asked while they washed their hands together in the strange trough-like basin running the length of the washroom.

"Of course." Tash's expression remained neutral.

"Don't you want to find your prince Tash?" Sophie asked softly.

"I think…I think mine got lost somewhere, I'm not holding my breath." Tash shrugged. "And neither should you. You need to get out there, have fun and stop thinking about romance, stop reading romance novels. They're giving you false expectations. All it will get you is disappointment."

"Maybe." Sophie conceded, purely to shut Tash up. Whatever Tash said Sophie would still hold out for something extraordinary. After what she'd been through she needed something special, someone who thought her special. And if she never found him, well she'd just have to remain single.

Better no relationship than a bad relationship.

She slipped back onto her cow-hide bar stool wondering whether to head back to Chalet Repos. But if she did, one of the guest's children would be bound to be having a don't-want-to-go-to-bed tantrum and she'd have to smile and pretend it was okay as she cleared up the latest mess they'd created, even though she wasn't technically on duty.

As a veteran chalet girl she knew you had to make yourself scarce during your free time or you'd fall prey to the "would you mind just's" and "if you've got a sec's".

"So, who's doing the Valentine's day Speed Ski Dating event?" Lucy asked.

"Yes, I'll be there. It was a laugh last year," Tash said loudly, drinking her cocktail as fast as if it were orange squash.

"I won't be going, because Matt will be out here. We're going to be busy and it's not as though I'm single anymore." Amelia turned to Sophie. "How about you?"

Sophie considered. She'd never met anyone yet in all the years she'd been coming to Verbier for the winter season. But what else was there for her to do? Hang around at the chalet being lumbered with extra child-care duties, feeling sorry for herself as she cleaned chocolate fingerprints off the windows.

"I suppose." Sophie grimaced. "Being single on Valentine's Day isn't much fun and I've got nothing better to do. I'm just not too sure you can make love happen by throwing a bunch people together and hoping they'll pair off."

"It is a bit random but you might meet someone." Amelia shrugged. "It happens."

Sophie was glad for Amelia, really she was, but there was a certain smugness about her smile that irritated her.

God, I'm being a bitch tonight.

Sophie picked up her drink, hoping it would help improve her mood and make her a little nicer.

"She's right you know, it might happen." Tash poked Sophie in the ribs. "Especially if you look for Mr. Now rather than Mr. Forever. You've got to lower your sights, Soph, have some fun."

"Hmm," Sophie replied noncommittally, draining her cocktail. Then she looked up, catching Luc's sympathetic grey eyes, and a fresh flush crept up the back of her neck.

"Do a lot of people go?" Lucy asked.

"You get a good crowd." Tash put her empty glass down on the bar. "Come on. Let's go to The Lodge and find some nice men to buy us drinks. I'm skint."

Sophie groaned inwardly. She hated cadging drinks, feeling obligated. Even worse she hated feeling like a piece of meat at a cattle market. What was the point of going to a hook-up bar when she didn't want a one-night stand?

I'm twenty-five, am I getting too old for this?

She enjoyed skiing and loved Switzerland. She felt truly happy in the mountains, enjoying the sun, snow and crisp Alpine air. It had always worked out perfectly for her, given Uncle Frank's café in the Lake District closed for the winter. Being a seasonaire suited her; that hadn't changed. But something else had.

Maybe she could slink back to the dorm room without anyone noticing and put her headphones on to drown out any tantrum noises. If the other three were out for the evening it would give her some quiet time to read. Without interruptions.

"I've got a bit of a headache, I'm going back to the chalet," she said, sliding off her stool and grabbing her bag.

Tash snorted again. "Back to Nathan?"

"Who's Nathan?" Amelia asked, confused.

"He's in the book she's reading," Tash explained. "But he's not going to keep her warm at night, is he? I'd take a real Pierre over a fictional Nathan any day, wouldn't you?"

"I've got my electric blanket to keep me warm, thanks," Sophie replied.

"And Pierre would probably hog the duvet." Lucy smiled at Sophie in a way that made Sophie feel maybe she had an ally after all.

Sophie recognised his voice from where she stood in the queue for a green armband. As if she could ever forget it. Surreptitiously she slunk to the back of the queue and edged away, hoping he

9

wouldn't see her, dread pumping through her body.

He probably doesn't even remember you.

She propped her skis up against a wall and leant against it herself for a minute, glad to feel the solid concrete behind her, even though it was freezing. Why was she even doing the Valentine Ski Dating event again? All so she could meet more jerks like Thomas?

She stared up at the snowy peaks and startlingly blue sky, scenery she normally loved but right now it couldn't distract her from the memory of another day in a queue for the chair-lift, imprinted into her brain with vivid clarity. It'd been the morning after her hideous mistake, her experiment at trying to be like everyone else, doing what everyone else was doing.

Having fun.

Except it hadn't been fun. Not even remotely.

Sophie squeezed her eyes tight shut as though she could squeeze the memory out of her mind. But it wasn't that easy and the wave of remembered humiliation passed over her, drenching her with fresh embarrassment at the memory. She couldn't stop the words from flooding her thoughts too – the words Thomas had used to describe their night together to his friends the next day in the queue for the ski lift.

'Always go for the overweight ones, lads. Fat girls try harder in bed.'

It'd been two years ago but he might as well have just said it. She didn't know what had been worse, those words or the look of pity in the eyes of his friend who had seen her first and had belatedly nudged Thomas to shut him up. Discovering afterwards that he and his friends held No Standards Wednesdays competitions, to see who could bag the biggest "minger" had been the ultimate humiliation. Although she couldn't be sure they'd done it that particular night they'd hooked up… Still the suspicion was enough to make her hate Thomas like she'd never hated another human being before. She was angry with herself too, for imagining a handsome, semi-professional skier had fancied her.

What really rankled was that she hadn't even been overweight, not medically anyway, although maybe by Verbier trustafarian standards. Technically she'd been a healthy weight for her height for almost the first time in years that season. But in two sentences he'd swept away any achievement she'd felt in her weight loss. It seemed she was always destined to be the fat girl. No matter how much weight she lost after that, a little bit of her always felt like the fat girl inside.

Tash had been wrong, it'd been two years since she'd had sex, not a year. There'd been a sweet guy she'd been friendly with last season but all they'd ever done was cuddled. He'd never tried to take it further and she'd been too scared of rejection to push it. God forbid she be seen to "try harder" again. Now she was afraid of trying at all. If she fancied anyone she kept it quiet.

Opening her eyes again she scanned the crowd in front of her. There was no sign of Thomas and his loud friends. It was safe to go ahead.

But do I really want to?

"Hey, there you are." Tash came up alongside her, already wearing a dark-green armband over the sleeve of her purple ski jacket. "Where did you get to? Why haven't you got your armband yet?"

"I'm just doing it." Sophie shuffled forward to join the end of the queue. This had to be better than spending Valentine's Day on her own, didn't it?

"Seen anyone you like the look of yet?" Tash joined her in the queue while Lucy went off to the lockers for her skis. For the first time that day Sophie noticed Tash's eye make-up, the dark-grey Kohl and deep-pink eye-shadow accentuating her cat like eyes, the same shade as the pink streaks in her fair hair. She looked beautiful, although a little scary. Sophie admired the men who had the courage to take her on.

"Hmm, not sure." Sophie looked half-heartedly around her. There were quite a few tourists in the crowd joining in the event and many were drinking openly or already drunk.

"Twats who fancy themselves as Johnny Depp," Tash sneered dismissively at a group of young men dressed up as pirates, already drunk and spraying each other with expensive champagne. "What a waste of Moët."

"Well they keep the rescue helicopters busy I 'spose." Sophie pursed her lips. Why did she always feel like a kill-joy lately? Jaded and cynical already, at twenty-five. She sighed, something was going to have to change.

Once she'd given her name and put her green armband on over her sleeve they headed back to find Lucy and clicked their skis on, heading for the start of the run.

"So how is this supposed to work exactly?" Lucy asked, glowering as one of the pirates cut her up and wolf-whistled.

"It's like a singles' bar on snow really – you see someone you like the look of, you go and say hello. And we all meet up at the mountain cantine at the next station for a drink. Then you ski to the next station and stop for a drink and so on. There'll be food too I think," Tash explained, casting a cool eye over the crowd around them. "You could accidentally ski into someone you fancy but really it's not advised, they're not going to be too keen on you if you've just broken their leg."

Sophie decided just to enjoy the run without even looking at the people around her. Every year so far she'd looked, been hopeful of catching someone's eye but being alone with her Kindle definitely seemed a better deal than landing up with the likes of Thomas. The only romance they knew was pretending to be charming until they'd actually got you into bed. Then they dropped the act.

Like kissing a prince only for him to turn into a frog. What's wrong with this picture?

She put her sunglasses on and as they set off down the slope she enjoyed the familiar buzz of speed, fresh air and fantastic scenery. She'd always loved sledging as a kid but this was way better. You had so much more control, once you'd got a bit of experience.

All around her she could see inexperienced skiers going far too fast and with little or no control. It took all her skill to avoid collisions with them.

Pulling up at the bottom of the slope and avoiding those whose skills clearly didn't include stopping without falling over, Sophie deliberately avoided catching anyone's eye. Which was why when someone skied directly in front of her and stopped suddenly, spraying snow up into the air she practically jumped out of her skies.

"Pardon Mademoiselle," the handsome skier said, his face stretched into a grin. His fair hair flopped down into startling blue eyes. "Sophie?"

"Er, oui?" Sophie replied, frowning slightly. How did this guy know her name? Then she noticed he didn't have a green armband on like the rest of them and felt more confused than ever. Was it one of the organisers?

"J'ai quelque chose pour vous." From inside his jacket he retrieved a red, heart-shaped card and he handed it to her. Before she could protest or ask who he was he'd skied off, down towards the next run.

"What did he give you?" Lucy asked. Both she and Tash snapped off their skis and crowded round her, peering over her shoulder.

Sophie showed them the heart-shaped card with Mme. Sophie written on the front. Then she turned it over and stared with astonishment at the writing on the back. "I think it's some kind of clue."

CHAPTER TWO

Bonjour chère Sophie, I'd love to meet,
Follow these clues for a special treat.
Clue one sings love songs, is a chairlift,
And a number you can eat.

Sophie stared hard at the words on the heart-shaped card.

"Is this a wind up?" She narrowed her eyes at Tash. This would be just the kind of thing she'd waste her time on.

"Hey, this nothing to do with me." Tash held up her gloved hands, palm side up. "Not guilty."

"Hmm." Sophie decided to reserve judgment. Tash was a good actress. Sophie had seen her lie with practiced ease on numerous occasions while they'd been working together.

And how could this possibly be real? Who would go to this kind of effort for me?

Her mind flickered over the ski-bum instructors they drank with. Definitely not their style. Most thought buying you a drink was all they had to do to get a girl into bed, or even into the loos on some occasions.

Hardly romantic.

Unbidden, a memory of Luc's dark eyes staring intently at her flickered into her mind.

Ridiculous. Of course he doesn't like me, he was just being kind.

She wouldn't let herself get caught up in this only to discover it was just a big joke at her expense. Another Valentine's Day loomed in her memory, an ugly spectre.

A warning.

She'd been only sixteen when she'd found a Valentine's card wedged in the corner of her school locker. She'd treasured it all day, sneaking peaks at the card where it lay between two exercise books in her school bag. For once she'd been able to ignore the muffled sniggers and taunts from the class bullies, clutching her delicious secret close to her like a protective shield. She even dared to hope it might be from Paul. She'd had a crush on him for...well forever. But all the girls fancied him, as captain of the football team he could pretty much take his pick from the pretty girls, the thin girls.

But a girl could hope, couldn't she?

When ringleader Clarissa had announced to the whole class at the end of the day that she'd sent it as a joke, well, the remembered humiliation could still make her crumple beneath its weight. Then had come the taunts – "Who'd send you a card then, Sophie?" "Maybe another fatty might take pity on you, you didn't think Paul had sent it, did you? What a scream!"

Screaming had been exactly what Sophie felt like doing. How had that witch Clarissa known she had a crush on Paul? Had her surreptitious glances in his direction been so obvious to everyone? Was he laughing at her too?

Ever since then she'd hated Valentine's Day with a vengeance.

"You look worried Soph." Lucy lightly touched her arm, drawing Sophie out from the shadow of the bad memories. "We'll come with you and help. I think it'll be great fun."

"Of course we're coming." Tash grinned. "We positively have a duty to go with her in case the guy's a nut job."

"Well, hang on, I'm not actually sure I..." Sophie felt a surge of anxiety at the speed things were moving. Shouldn't she think this through a bit more?

"Not that he's any more likely to be a nut job than any of these guys." Tash waved a hand to gesture towards the other skiers coming down for the first planned stop of the day. She appeared not to have heard Sophie's protest.

Resistance with Tash was useless once she'd got a project to fixate on. Although if she was going to follow this clue it would be nice to have some company.

"But, don't you want to carry on with the ski-dating schedule?" Sophie hesitated, brain still trying to make sense of this. She couldn't really have a secret admirer, could she?

"Nah, I don't have problems meeting men. Anyway if there's anyone interesting here we'll catch up with them at the drinks later on, eh, Lucy?" Tash's eyes sparkled with a confidence Sophie envied.

"Yes of course, I wouldn't miss this for anything. I've never had anyone go to these lengths for me." Lucy looked wistful.

At that moment the group dressed as pirates hurtled down the slope towards them, singing "We are pirates on the piste."

"On the piss more like." Tash yelled back and Sophie laughed, relaxing.

"Hey girls, fancy a shag?" A Johnny Depp wannabe shouted over at them.

"Oh please, is that really the best you can do?" Lucy's tone was scathing as she rolled her eyes, turning her back to them.

Sophie laid a restraining hand on Tash's forearm, having seen the flash of fight in her eyes. She could really do without the hassle. "Leave it," she whispered. "Let's just ignore them and concentrate on the clue. Please?"

After a moments deliberation Tash nodded her agreement, turning her attention back to the red card. "Amelia is going to be so gutted that she missed this."

"I think she's too busy being loved up with Matt to be bothered," Sophie replied. "She'll have met him off the plane at Geneva by now."

"So, we're working out the clue then and going ahead with this?" Lucy practically bounced up and down on the spot, her cheeks pink. "It's so romantic, you are lucky, Sophie."

"Erm, I suppose so." Sophie still wasn't sure this wasn't a giant wind-up and was trying to ignore the tiny flutter of hope battling for her attention. "But we might not be able to work it out. How can you eat a number that sings love songs?"

They all studied the card, ignoring the mêlée around them.

"Don't forget the chairlift bit. Maybe we should start with that?" Tash said.

"I think I read something in a magazine about chairlifts named after celebs here in Verbier," Lucy said, frowning, her petite features screwed up in concentration.

"I just get on the things. I don't hang about waiting to be introduced." Tash snorted.

"You know, I think Lucy is right. I vaguely remember seeing something about that online. We could look it up. I can just about pick up the café's free wifi from here." Sophie pulled her iPhone out from the inside pocket of her ski jacket.

She typed "Verbier chairlifts named after celebrities" into the search engine and positioned herself so both Tash and Lucy could see the screen. While waiting for the results to load she stamped her feet on the snow in an attempt to warm them up. A cloud covered the sun, making it too cold to stand still for long.

"Well, I don't think it's Diana Ross, although she does sing love songs," Tash said as they scanned the list of results.

"But she hasn't got a food connection, has she?" Sophie frowned and clicked on a different link. "Ooh, look, what about James Blunt, he has that restaurant, La Vache, doesn't he, with a couple of other celebs? And it says here he's got a chairlift named after him. I've never been to the restaurant, have you?"

"It's a bit pricy, it's not like we can afford to be regulars there, is it?" Tash replied. "But maybe we could stretch to sharing a pizza."

Tash and Lucy snapped their skis back on, but Sophie hesitated, catching Lucy's eye. Lucy shrugged as though to say "Why not?"

Why not? It's not as though I've got anything better to do today.

"Come on you two," Tash called out. "We've got a chairlift to queue for."

Deep down Sophie knew she really wanted to do this but it was as though a part of her refused to believe the excitement, too afraid of the possible crash waiting for her ahead. She was afraid to jump, afraid this run might end in painful disaster and public humiliation.

But what if this wasn't a joke? What if her secret Valentine was someone who actually liked her?

Careful, Soph, this could be a wind-up. Don't get your hopes up.

Still she followed Tash and Lucy and they skied alongside her, skillfully avoiding the novices' crash landings into the snowdrifts. Lucy was a good skier considering this was her first season. She was easily as good as them already, if not better.

As they travelled up in the chairlift it became apparent why the restaurant was called La Vache. Several life-sized fake cows stood outside the entrance.

Sophie peered inside; it was chalet chic at its finest, a mixture of bare wood and cow-hide rugs. Fur throws hung over the chairs. It was far smarter than the mountain cantines they occasionally ate lunch at. Getting free food at Chalet Repos meant they usually saved their money for drinks and going out.

"Hey, come and have a look at this," Lucy called out, her voice rising in excitement.

Sophie and Tash hurried over to where Lucy stood pointing to a board displaying the restaurant menu.

"Look at number nine, it's a James Blunt pizza," Lucy announced. "So we must've got the clue right; it all works out."

"So what do I have to do now?" Sophie stared at the menu, bemused.

"Go in and order it," Tash said. "We can share it."

Sophie hovered near the entrance, still undecided, when a waiter came out.

"Mademoiselle Sophie, nous avons une table pour vous. Vous êtes trois?" He asked.

"Oui trois, merci. Mais..." Sophie's objection was ignored by everyone as Lucy and Tash followed the waiter inside. Sophie held back, suddenly plagued by the idea that this wasn't a wind-up but mistaken identity. Had she taken the clue meant for some other Sophie? Maybe the guy who delivered the card got her mixed up with someone else.

"Apparently we can have a pizza each on the house," Tash announced with satisfaction, once Sophie had caught up with them at the table. The table had been laid for four but one set of plates and cutlery was discreetly whisked away.

How had whoever set the clue known she wouldn't come on her own? But then not many women would go to meet a stranger without some kind of support or back up, especially if they didn't know anything about him. It must be someone who knew her fairly well, but hadn't realised Amelia would be off with Matt in Geneva today.

"They said that? But why?" Sophie dropped her voice to a whisper. "You know, now I think about it I'm sure this isn't meant for me, they must've got the wrong Sophie. I have to check, I'm not sure I can afford to pay for a full meal today once they find out I'm the wrong Sophie."

Tash stared at her, incredulous. "Just eat the free pizza. If they've made a mistake that's their problem."

"How do they know you are anyway?" Lucy frowned. "And the guy who delivered the first card, how did he know it was you? Have you ever met him?"

"No, not that I remember. Excusez moi Monsieur," Sophie called out to the waiter. "Could you just tell me how you know my name?"

The waiter tapped the side of his nose, a gesture that irritated Sophie.

"Seriously, I need to know." Sophie stared back, determined

not to eat a mouthful until she knew the free pizza was really intended for her.

"Ici." The waiter reached in his pocket for his phone and showed her a photograph on the screen.

It was Sophie's Facebook photograph.

"Oh, I see, thank you." Sophie bit her lip and picked up a menu. "Well I'd better order a number nine pizza then, the James Blunt one. What are you both having?"

She knew she sounded decisive and in control but inside she was in turmoil. Who could be doing this for her? It was an elaborate and expensive joke, if that was what it was, or maybe...

She tuned out the girls' orders, deep in thought as they chatted. When the waiter returned with some bread he had another red, heart-shaped card in his hand.

Tash grabbed it enthusiastically and passed it to Sophie. She turned it over on the table so they could all see the words.

It's nice, ice to be romantic,
Don't you think?
You'll find clue two here,
At a cool place to drink.
P.S. When you ask for this clue
Remember to wink!

Sophie knew the answer instantly this time. "It's The Ice Cube, has to be."

Tash nodded, her fingers seemed reluctant to relinquish the card to Sophie.

"Will they be open this afternoon?" Lucy asked. "I've only ever been in the evening."

"Only one way to find out, once we've had our pizza we'll head off, we can ski down to there from here I think." Tash turned to face Sophie. "Have you still no idea who's behind this? He certainly knows his Verbier. Even we didn't know about the chairlift."

Sophie had thought that too. Tash was a good actress but not this good surely? Who else would do this and what were their intentions?

"I still can't shake the feeling this is a massive wind up." Sophie moved back in her chair to give the waiter room to put their pizzas down. The food looked good and suddenly she felt ravenous.

"Wind up or not we've been given free food." Tash said, tucking in.

"Mmm, this is nice," Lucy said, doing likewise.

Sophie picked up her knife and fork and ate.

"Whatever happened to that guy, Thomas, wasn't it? Didn't you and he have a thing together the first season I was out here? Maybe it's him doing this?" Tash suggested and Sophie almost choked on her mouthful.

"Not a thing exactly," Sophie replied, staring down at her plate.

"So you don't think it could be him?" Tash persisted.

"No." Sophie gave a snort of laughter, the very idea of Thomas as a romantic utterly ludicrous.

"He wasn't romantic then?" Lucy asked, curiously.

"Most definitely not." Sophie attacked her pizza and wouldn't meet their eyes.

"What about that guy last year, I forget his name." Tash frowned.

"No, it's not Will either." Sophie replied tersely. "Look I honestly have no idea who's behind it, okay?"

Both Tash and Lucy fell quiet, unused to Sophie snapping. Good old Sophie was reliable, nice and even-tempered. Sophie caught the raised eyebrows and felt a pang of guilt.

"Look I'm sorry, I didn't mean to snap." This time she did meet their eyes. "I really do appreciate you both coming with me, it's just my dating history hasn't been all that great, you know? Thomas is a bastard and William, well, he's about as romantic as a wet lettuce. So I'm just hoping my luck is about to change."

Lucy smiled sympathetically. "Hey, we've all had our share of bad luck but you never know, let's enjoy today and see what happens, keep an open mind, okay?"

As policies went it was a good one, but years of protecting herself from disappointment seemed to have taken their toll. Part of her wanted to go back to Chalet Repos and curl up with her Kindle. So much safer. In control.

On the way to the Ice Cube bar Sophie had to swerve to avoid a small girl with blonde plaits lying in the snow and crying her eyes out, calling for her Maman.

Only once she'd picked the girl back up onto her skies, soothed her and reunited her with her mother did Sophie go to join Tash and Lucy, waiting in the sun outside the Ice Cube Bar for her. The clouds had vanished, leaving the pistes bathed in warm sunshine, the snow sparkling and shimmering in the light. The terrace was almost full with skiers, drinks in hand, sunbathing and drinking in the view.

"You're really good with kids, Soph," Tash said as they deposited their ski gear in the racks outside.

"No, seriously, I've seen you with the little brats staying at the moment. Personally I'd like to throttle them but you seem to have the knack." Tash headed to the bar.

Sophie followed her, trying to fight the intense swell of emotion rising dangerously high. She just hoped her inner flood defences could hold it back, otherwise she was afraid the pain might sweep her away.

"Are you okay, Sophie?" Lucy spoke softly, her eyes full of concern.

Lucy doesn't miss much.

For one brief moment Sophie considered confiding but...well, she hadn't told anyone yet, not even her parents. The horrible secret had created a barrier around her. It protected her but it also made a prisoner of her and she didn't know what would happen if she broke it down.

"Yeah, I'm okay. So, do you think I'm actually supposed to wink when we order the drinks?" Sophie attempted to sound composed, forcing a smile to her face. "What if they've got no idea what I'm on about? We could have the clue wrong after all."

Icy-cold fingers of panic gripped at her chest as they approached the bar.

What if the barman thinks I'm coming on to him?

"I can do it if you like?" Tash suggested.

"I think it probably has to be Sophie," Lucy said and Tash shrugged.

Great, another opportunity to make myself a laughing stock.

Sophie mentally put on her big-girl pants and approached the bar to get on with it, forcing a wide smile to her face.

"Bonjour. Can I ask you, do you, erm, have something for me?" Her voice could barely be heard over the loud, pulsing music. Heat flooded her cheeks. Then, feeling Tash's elbow poking into her ribs she abandoned her reserve and winked at the barman, waiting for him to look at her with disdain.

But instead he smiled back at her. "Sophie?"

She nodded.

"Yes, I have something for you. If you go up to the terrace I will bring it up."

They went up to join the sunbathers and some of the tension left Sophie's taut muscles. The sky was a vivid blue against the dramatic white peaks and the sun warm on her face, soothing and caressing her. Sophie loved the Swiss winter sunshine. You couldn't sunbathe in the Lake District in winter. In Coniston she'd be permanently swathed in layers of fleece and Gortex to protect her from the relentless onslaught of a fell winter. You certainly couldn't sit out in the sun in an English winter.

When the barman came up to find them he had a tray of champagne flutes as well as the red, heart-shaped card they'd been expecting.

"The drinks are already paid for," the barman said as he deposited the flutes on to a low wooden table in front of them. Tash and Lucy grabbed the champagne first but Sophie picked up the card, trying not to look too eager. She turned it over and put it on the table so the clue was visible to the other two.

> *Can you hear bells?*
> *It's clue number three,*
> *To get this one*
> *You must ask for a key.*
> *P.S. If you've still no idea*
> *Ask Scott or Holly!*

"Scott and Holly? Are they a part of this too?" Lucy voiced the question also on Sophie's mind.

"Oh I get it," Tash said, sitting back in her chair, smiling with cat-like satisfaction as she sipped her champagne. She often reminded Sophie of a cat – just as likely to pounce on her prey as she was to purr and rub against your legs.

"So?" Lucy asked. "Aren't you going to tell us?"

"I think Sophie can get this one without our help," Tash said, her smile stretching into a grin. "Well this must be someone we know, if he knows Holly and Scott."

"Everyone in Verbier knows Holly and Scott." Sophie replied absently, still thinking about the bells. Then the mention of Holly and Scott jogged her memory. "Oh, I get it."

"Will someone please tell me?" Lucy leant forward in her seat, frowning.

"It's the wedding chapel," Sophie explained before Tash could wind Lucy up any further. "Scott and Holly got married there. Holly did arrange a few weddings there too with a ski and winter wonderland theme. I think she found it too much, though, there haven't been any this season. I didn't like to ask, it all got rather fraught."

"The girl you replaced, Lucy, her name was Amy. She ran off with the groom for the first wedding, so it never actually happened." Tash arched her eyebrows expressively.

"Oh?" Lucy's sharp eyes gleamed with interest.

"Tash!" Sophie frowned. "That's not very fair, Josh, the groom turned out to be Amy's ex and his bride-to-be was...difficult."

"Sophie means the bride was a total bitch," Tash translated. "Now calm down, Soph, Amy's my friend, I'm not judging her, you should know me better than that. I'm just filling Lucy in on the details. Maybe they'll be important for this treasure hunt."

"Yeah, right." Sophie stared at Tash suspiciously. Her cat-like eyes stared back, opaque, giving nothing away.

"So, how do we get to the church, then?" Lucy asked, breaking the tense silence. "And what's all this about a key?"

"You can get a key from the Tourist Information Centre," Sophie said, glad that this clue was easy to solve at least.

She drank the champagne, hoping the explosion of bubbles on her tongue might take the edge off her unease. Tash going on about children had plunged her into the blackest of moods. She rarely cried, never unburdened herself to the other girls, preferring to provide the shoulder to cry on, to solve the problems of others rather than gaze at her own navel.

Good old Sophie, always dependable, a safe pair of hands.

But what would they say if they knew everything about her? A lurch of panic turned her insides topsy-turvy. Thankfully she was good at hiding her emotions. Years of being bullied at school had taught her to hide the emotions the bullies feasted on, hungry to draw a reaction from her.

Withdrawing deep inside herself was a habit she couldn't imagine ever breaking.

"How many clues will there be do you think?" Lucy mused.

"I don't know but we're certainly doing okay out of it, this is the good stuff." Tash nodded at the champagne flutes, now virtually empty.

Maybe Tash and Lucy would prefer it if they got going. After all they would probably want to catch the end of the ski-dating event. They were missing it because of her.

"Shall we get going?" She stood up, draining the last of her champagne. A pleasant warmth spread through her chest and her cheeks flushed with heat from a combination of alcohol and the warm Swiss sunshine.

They made it to the tourist office without any problems and the friendly brunette behind the desk smiled warmly at Sophie, a knowing look shining in her eyes. Sophie wished she knew who was behind this. Thoughts of Luc flitted into her kind from time to time but she batted them away.

He's out of my league. Haven't you learnt your lesson since Thomas? Or since Paul at school? Fancying the cool guys only got her into trouble.

The tiny stone chapel sat at the top of the slope, stark and beautiful against the now-changing backdrop of sky. Soft amber light glowed on the mountaintops as the sun prepared to sink down below the peaks. The slanting light made everything look beautiful. Golden.

Sophie felt surprisingly emotional as she opened the door to the chapel, remembering Holly and Scott's wedding. She'd been so glad when they got it together. They now both seemed so much more...peaceful somehow. It was hard to define the contended vibe she felt in their presence.

With a stab of longing and loneliness she suddenly desperately wanted that for herself. The desire was a sharp throbbing pain in her chest. Only by making a conscious effort to relax her muscles could she breathe deeply again.

She walked up the small aisle, it only took a few strides. When Tash followed her singing 'here comes the bride' Sophie felt an uncharacteristic urge to throttle her. Instead she kept a stiff back as the better option.

Is Tash being more Tashy than usual or is it me? Perhaps it's just my dark mood casting shadows over everything, making it impossible to see things clearly?

She softened towards Tash, remembering all the times she'd been a good friend to her and all the laughs they'd had together. Maybe Tash was a bit off today too; Valentine's Day could do that to a single girl. Sophie didn't think Tash had received any Valentine's cards or she would've showed them all at breakfast.

Sophie's eye was caught by a flash of red lying on the lectern. She extracted the card gently, reverently, determined to show respect while they were here. Who had persuaded the woman in the tourist office to allow this? Had the spirit of Valentine's Day infected everyone?

"Let's go outside to read it." Tash shuddered. "This place gives me the willies."

Lucy and Sophie followed her outside and they stood close together to read the card, their breath now showing as vapour clouds in the cooling air.

A house of rest is clue number four,
You'll find it pinned to the front of the door.
Now you've got the final clue,
We get to the bit where I meet you.

Sophie felt an involuntary thrill run through her at the idea of actually meeting whoever had set this all up. Then her stomach flipped and she felt sick. She could only hope if she was heading for a fall it wouldn't be a humiliating public one.

Fat chance of that.

"A house of rest, does that mean a tomb or a funeral home or something?" Lucy screwed her face up in concentration.

"No, I don't think so," Sophie said slowly. "I think it means Chalet Repos."

"So Holly and Scott must be in on it," Lucy exclaimed.

"If we're right," Tash said. "Well there's only one way to find out. I can't wait to see who's behind this."

Sophie hesitated, really wanting to do the last clue on her own. Could she politely tell them to bog off? Maybe not. It might be better if she explained that she really needed to end this without any onlookers. At least that way she could minimise any potential humiliation.

This still could turn out to be a joke. Albeit an elaborate, expensive one.

When they walked towards Chalet Repos carrying their skis Sophie searched eagerly for a familiar flash of red. There it was, another red heart-shaped card attached to the front door.

She increased her pace, almost going flying on a piece of black ice on the pavement. Tash and Lucy hurried to keep up with her. On the front door the heart card bore her name in familiar handwriting. She tugged it free from the piece of tape and eagerly turned it over.

W is your final clue,
Be there at eight and I'll find you.
Now it's time for us to meet,
Have a cocktail or two and something to eat.
A bientôt Sophie.

The W!

Tash caught up behind her and whistled. "Do you know how much cocktails cost at the W?"

"I'm guessing a lot?" Sophie hadn't been inside the brand-new hotel development yet but she'd gazed with longing from the outside. She'd even googled the Living Room and it all looked amazing. Not to mention way out of their price range.

She fished her phone out of her coat pocket to check the time. Good, she should have time to get the dinner on for the guests and work out what on earth she was going to wear.

In the corridor they bumped into Holly.

"So, who's Sophie's secret Valentine then, Holly?" Tash demanded before Holly even had a chance to say hello. "Spill."

"Certainly not." Holly smiled. "My lips are sealed, I wouldn't ruin the surprise for anything but I think you're in for a treat Sophie."

"Oh, I..." Sophie tailed off. Holly wouldn't be involved in a joke at her expense, she was far too kind.

This is real.

Heat flushed across her face, she turned to Tash and Lucy. "Don't you two want to get off to the drinks for the ski-dating event?"

"And miss seeing who this Secret Valentine guy is?" Tash said. "What if he's an axe-murderer? We should go along to protect you."

"He's not an axe-murderer and they're meeting in a public place," Holly said firmly, slipping her arm through Sophie's. "I think Sophie can take it from here on her own. Now Sophie, what are you going to wear? Would you like to borrow a dress?

CHAPTER THREE

Thank goodness for Holly. Not only had she lent Sophie the loveliest clingy jersey dress in a flattering dark-plum shade but she'd even taken over Sophie's dinner duty for her so she had more time to get ready.

The dress felt comfortable yet also looked smart, especially with the tan-leather knee-high boots Lucy had lent her. It felt nice to be dressed up for a change and out of her usual jeans and hoodie combo.

Holly did her best by threat and inducement to prevent Tash from tailing Sophie to the W.

Approaching the new hotel development Sophie didn't feel nearly fortified enough by the crème de cassis she'd hurriedly drunk back at Chalet Repos. She felt a little daunted by the Porche Cayennes and Aston Martins driving into the hotel's underground car park. Some of the guests walking into the hotel looked like their outfit cost more than her entire annual salary. Having seen the price of the clothing in the Verbier boutiques she was probably right.

She stepped out of the cold night air into the lobby, immediately warmed by the line of artificial flames flickering the whole length of the space. Music pumped out from the cocktail bar down to the left while on the right guests with expensive-looking luggage checked in. Sophie stared, confused, unsure where to go. There were no obvious lifts or helpful signs to restaurants.

Help.

"Can I help you?" A polite male voice behind her made her jump. It was almost as though he'd heard her silent plea.

Sophie turned and started at the sight of a very attractive, chisel-jawed man who looked like he modeled for Abercrombie and Fitch in his spare time. Her heart beat faster.

Was this her Secret Valentine? Surprisingly, despite the fact he was gorgeous, she felt her spirits dip in disappointment.

I was still hoping it might be Luc; how stupid of me.

But this alternative seemed equally unlikely.

"Hi, I'm..." Sophie stopped when she saw the large 'W' on the guy's trendy red scarf. This was the doorman? "I'm meeting someone, for cocktails I think, or the restaurant...I'm not sure where I'm meeting...my friend."

I can't say I don't know who I'm meeting.

Now she looked round all the staff seemed equally gorgeous. She was in the presence of The Beautiful People.

The door man's warm smile increased in wattage. "You are Mademoiselle Sophie, yes?"

"Yes, I am," she said, feeling as though she were in a very strange dream. Perhaps she'd wake and find the whole of the Valentine hunt had been nothing but a dream! If this wasn't a dream it looked a great deal like how she imagined heaven – stylish and beautiful with soft lighting and chill-out music. Staffed by gorgeous, smiling angels... If she were designing heaven she'd certainly make it like this.

"Come with me." The model slash doorman walked down towards The Living Room and Sophie followed, feeling as different to the people around her as though she were still wearing her jeans and hoodie. Her heart rate increased, pounding a steady thrum in her temples.

If someone wants to make a fool of me this would be a good

place to do it.

But surely she'd abandoned the wind-up theory? Who would go to these lengths to humiliate her?

Who would go to these lengths to woo you either?

Both possibilities seemed equally unlikely, if she was honest with herself.

Then she remembered Holly again. Holly would never be involved in anything that would hurt her, she was sure of it.

"I'll leave you here," the doorman said, smiling cheerfully, as though they were old friends, before he turned and left.

The flashing lights and chrome bar top momentarily distracted Sophie as she stared around at the ultra-modern decor. There were lots of bed-like seating areas dotted around the room, all covered with cosy-looking faux-fur rugs and cushions. She couldn't see anyone she knew. Should she make a dash for the loos? Or go and wait on the balcony, maybe? She could see glass Perspex swing seats out there, complete with more fur throws and soft cushions.

At least she could see a clear route to the balcony. The loos were nowhere in sight and would require tracking down another member of staff. Just as she was about to make her way across the room she heard someone speak her name over the sound of the slowly pulsing beat of the music.

She spun around, heart leaping wildly as she found herself staring up into Luc's grey eyes.

He wore a dark charcoal suit and crisp white shirt with no tie. His grey eyes focused on her with an intensity that made her shiver. The only thing still remotely scruffy about him was his out-of-control dark hair, flopping this way and that as though it had a will of its own.

"Have you had a good day?" He asked, eyes crinkling a little with amusement.

What if he's here to meet someone else? Does he know about the clues? Or did he set them...for me?

"Er, yes thank you." Sophie just about remembered to smile

back, determined not to be caught assuming he was here for her, although of course she hoped... "And you, are you here with someone?"

"Yes," Luc replied and Sophie sagged, hope draining slowly out of her body.

I told you not to get your hopes up.

Until that moment she hadn't let herself fully acknowledge her theory that this might be Luc, determined to show her that romance was alive and well; a huge stand on her behalf that would show her cynical friends.

"Oh." She turned her face away, not wanting him to see the disappointment she was sure was scrawled across her face, but her feet seemed unwilling to move.

"I'm with you, Sophie." Luc reached out and gently touched the side of her face. Her skin burned at his touch, sending a fresh flush across her face and neck.

"Oh." She turned her face back towards him, her mouth opened. His finger trailed along her jawline, grazing her lips and resting on her bottom lip. Desire stirred deep inside her, licking at her and turning her to jelly.

Luc withdrew his hand.

"So it was you today? Those clues?" she asked. It was as though she still didn't dare believe it might be true. She needed him to spell it out for her.

"Yes," Luc said simply.

"Thank you." She looked away, glad at this point that a waiter arrived to hand Luc some cocktail menus.

Thank you?

Sophie cringed inwardly at her choice of words, feeling horribly self-conscious as Luc handed her one of the menus. Her eyes popped at the prices. She'd been right to assume she couldn't afford this place. She gazed at the listed ingredients for each cocktail. They all looked delicious.

"The Royal Framboise sounds heavenly." Sophie read the list of ingredients from the menu, forgetting to be self-conscious. "Fresh raspberries, slices of ginger, raspberry liquor over ice and topped by champagne."

"Would you like one?" Luc smiled. "Maybe I should expand my cocktail menu at Bar des Amis."

"Oh, yes please, I'd love one, thank you." Sophie smiled, relaxing.

Are you ever going to say anything that isn't please or thank you?

But being this close to Luc, without a solid bar between them felt...disconcerting.

"Where would you like to sit?" Luc asked.

Sophie thought about it. There was somewhere she'd been dying to visit in the hotel. "Do you think we could take them across to that room where the seats go all the way up the stairs and there's a huge plate-glass window looking out at the view? You know, the room with the red lights. I've seen it on the internet."

"Sure, whatever you like, we've got at least thirty minutes until our table reservation at the Arola restaurant."

When Luc had placed their order they had made their way through the doors opposite the bar that led to the red room and climbed to a pair of seats halfway up the stairs.

As they settled down to wait for their drinks, Luc turned to Sophie.

"So, did you really have a nice day?" He reached out and tucked a stray hair behind her ear. His fingers brushed her skin lightly, making her fizz.

She definitely approved of this touching thing, she hoped there was going to be a whole lot more of it. She was just about to answer him when the waiter appeared at the bottom of the space, carrying a tray with their cocktails.

He placed them on the small table that was part of the unit between their two seats. Sophie stared at the small dish made of ice containing raspberries that floated on the top of her tall glass.

Once the waiter had retreated she carefully lifted the drink and sat back a little, sipping at it. Instantly the fresh raspberries and ginger overwhelmed her taste buds.

So this is what money tastes like – heaven.

Yet she couldn't let herself be seduced entirely. She'd fallen for Thomas, after all, and the smooth moves and lies he'd used to bait his line before reeling her in, hook line and sinker. And all the time he'd been laughing at her.

"Sophie? You were about to tell me about your day?" Luc's voice interrupted her thoughts and she cursed herself for letting Thomas into her thoughts. He wasn't going to spoil this evening for her.

"Er yes," she swallowed a piece of crushed ice and coughed. "It was all so very...unexpected."

"And kind," she added, feeling suddenly ungrateful. "It was so kind of you to do all that."

Is that why he did this? To be kind? Perhaps it was his way of standing up for me, showing Tash and the others...what exactly? But then what's all the touching about?

Why did her thoughts feel like fighting through treacle? Still her head swam with questions she didn't dare utter as she stared down at her frosted glass, warmth from the liqueur spreading through her chest.

"Sophie?" Luc's musical way of saying her name with his French accent caused desire to stir inside her like a hibernating creature waking from a long sleep.

The creature didn't give a stuff about Luc's motives so long as he touched her again. She dared to look up, to meet his eyes, ready to stand up for herself if she met any hint of mockery in his eyes.

Instead she saw the intensity of darkening pupils and her slumbering desire roared into life, sending sexual electricity crackling through her, electrifying her nerve endings. Heat crept back into her cheeks and she was afraid that combined with the red lighting she must be the colour of her plum dress.

"I didn't do it to be kind. I admit I thought it might be..." he seemed to be searching for the correct English word, "satisfying to imagine the expression on your cynical friends' faces but that was just a bonus. I did it because I like you and I'd like to know you better."

"Do you do it for everyone you want to know better?" she asked.

"No," he replied simply and stared intently at her.

Sophie found she was leaning towards him, as though magnetised, her body acting without her consent, desperate to be closer to him.

"I'd like that too," she said quietly.

Great, now my mind has switched allegiances too.

Falling for him felt delicious but dangerous.

She was done for.

She stared at the triangle of flesh exposed at Luc's neck and the dark chest hair just visible. An x-rated fantasy of exactly how they might get to know each other played itself in her mind like a highly erotic film sequence. Sophie felt sure he could read her mind as their eyes locked, her desires reflected in his own eyes.

A shiver of excitement travelled up her spine.

He likes me, he likes me not. He likes me...

As he leant towards her her lips parted instinctively. Then a sudden fear that maybe he'd just been leaning forward to say something, not in fact kiss her entered her thoughts.

Oh crap, I'm no good at this, I'm too out of practice, this is too...

The icy, fearful dread melted the second his warm lips met hers, his tongue fleetingly pressing into her mouth, tasting of champagne.

When Sophie opened her eyes she caught sight of a waiter standing discreetly to one side, waiting patiently with some menus. She pulled back, embarrassed, trying to compose herself but sure they both saw her fingers tremble as she took the menu. That they were all bathed in red light made it all feel a bit surreal.

She barely heard the waiter's spiel about the menu, staring furiously out at the twinkling lights through the large plate-glass window facing the view.

"So, Sophie," Luc said once the waiter had left. "Tell me, when you're not in Verbier where do you disappear to? Where do you spend your summers?"

As Luc listened to Sophie tell him about her uncle's cafe in the Lake District he was glad to see her relax. Her shy smiles told him he'd done the right thing. He hadn't meant to kiss her, to move so fast, but she'd been utterly irresistible. Her soft pink lips practically begging to be kissed, parting for him. Yet he'd also sensed her hesitancy, a fear that needed to be coaxed away.

There was far more to Sophie than met the eye, but he guessed few people ever got to see beneath the surface.

"You know, I grew up working in my father's cafe, in a village called Vex up in the mountains. It sounds like we have a lot in common." He smiled at her. "Did you understand what the waiter was explaining about the menu?"

She stared at him blankly and then back down at the menu on her lap as though she'd forgotten its presence.

"It's basically a sharing menu," he explained. "It's not the traditional starter, main course and desert structure. We order lots of dishes at the same time and try new things. It's fun to do something different now and again, don't you agree?"

"New things sounds great to me." Sophie cleared her throat, then she picked up her cocktail and downed the last of it. She smiled and shrugged. "Sorry, I don't get to do this very often, I feel a bit..."

"Hey, relax," he reached out and squeezed her hand. "Would another cocktail help?"

She grinned, nodding. "You know me so well."

Somehow he felt he did, from their similar backgrounds he knew she was no stranger to hard work, family loyalty, their love of the mountains...

He ordered another Royal Framboise and as they walked through to the Arola restaurant he encouraged Sophie to talk about her life in the Lake District. When she talked about what she loved her eyes sparkled and lost their wariness. He found her hesitancy bewitchingly attractive. He'd seen her in action taking care of the novice chalet girl. She always did a fantastic job. Scott and Holly had great respect for her. So why didn't she have the same confidence in herself?

"I'd thought it might be a joke, you know." She said shyly once their dishes arrived on the table.

"A joke?" He frowned, puzzled.

"You know, er rigole?" She floundered. "Sorry, your English is so much better than my French."

"I spent a few years in London, I'd thought I wanted to live in a city but I missed the mountains too much to stay." He stared at her. "I know what the word 'joke' means. I'm just a little confused. Why would it be a joke?"

"I know it must seem odd but well, I once got a Valentine's card that was just that and I fell for it." Sophie blushed again, her blue eyes full of emotion. "But I'm being stupid, it was such a long time ago."

He reached across the table to hold her hand again, lightly stroking his thumb along her palm.

"A joke? People can be really cruel. Please don't think of it, Sophie. You are here, now, forget about the past," he said softly as he continued to caress her hand.

"Okay, I will." She smiled, her expression suddenly wistful, hungry even.

"Will you come home with me?" Luc cursed himself for letting the question slip out. He really had meant to take this slow but there was something about her that was simply irresistible and he was sure she felt the same.

This is special. Sophie is special.

She opened her mouth and then closed it again, blushing.

"Sorry," he said. "I didn't plan to say that. Forget I said anything, no pressure, okay?"

"But I'd like to come with you," she said quietly, meeting his eye.

That took him by surprise.

"That would be great." He squeezed her hand. "If you're sure?"

"I am."

The walk back to Bar des Amis felt magical. The surface of the snow sparkled as though scattered with tiny diamonds and above them the cloudless night revealed a sky full of twinkling stars.

Luc held Sophie's hand tightly, he couldn't wait to make love to her, to show her just how special she was.

Sophie's heart beat hard as they entered Bar des Amis. Luc unlocked the door and led her behind the bar. She followed him upstairs to his flat, practically fizzing with cocktails and erotic anticipation, her heart pounding hard. She wanted to tell him, to show him how much she liked him. To let him know how blown away she was by what he'd done for her today, the trouble he'd taken. But with every step closer to Luc's flat, closer to sex, Thomas' words reverberated through her mind.

Fat girls try harder.

"Is anything wrong?" Luc stopped as they came into the hallway of his flat and pulled her close to him, staring intently into her eyes.

His own eyes were dark, dilating pupils turning them the colour of charcoal. Soft light from a Verbier street light outside cast shadows in the hallway, bathing them in soft amber light.

"No, I want this, I really do. I just feel a bit...out of practice." Sophie bit her lip but forced herself to keep eye contact. Something about Luc made her feel she could trust him, made her want to let down the barriers and be truly naked in front of him, not clutching her secrets to her like covers that would shield her.

To trust him.

Fool, you know you can't trust anyone, not really. If you don't hold back you're going to get hurt.

But what if it wasn't like that this time?

It's always like that.

"There's nothing to be afraid of, Sophie." Luc placed a hand on her hip, his fingers warm and reassuring through the fabric of her dress.

There it was, the magically lyrical pronouncement of her name that turned her insides molten. She sighed softly, anxiety and tension ebbing from her body.

No overthinking. No objections. I don't care.

She wanted this whatever the consequences.

"Would you say that again? My name, I mean. I love the way you say my name." Sophie stared at Luc's mouth, remembering what it felt like to be kissed by him back at the W in the red room. As they stared at each other the space between them seemed to disappear, the world around them shrinking and slipping away.

All there is, is here and now. It's all that matters.

"Sophie." Luc smiled sexily, edging her up against the wall. The plaster felt solid behind her back and she inhaled his masculine, citrus-y scent, her senses overwhelmed.

"Je te veux," His whispered words against her ear tickled her skin, making it tingle, releasing darts of desire through her nervous system. His hot lips on her neck almost made her knees buckle. She was glad of the solid wall behind her, supporting her.

"Sexy Sophie, what would you like me to do to you?" Luc grinned slowly, sexily, sending warmth through her as his gaze travelled over her body, making her tingle from top to toe.

"Everything," she whispered. "I want you to do everything."

She meant it too. She'd never wanted sex like this, she wasn't sure she'd ever kissed a man like Luc before – sexy as hell but trustworthy.

Please God, let him be trustworthy.

His grin widened at her answer and he grasped her wrists, holding them high above her head, pressing them against the wall. The movement made her breasts rise up and press together, thrusting towards Luc. Her nipples hardened, pointing towards him through the lace of her bra and the jersey fabric of the dress. He held her wrists in place with one hand while the other skimmed her body, brushing lightly over her stiffening nipples and then dipping down between her legs. They kissed, his tongue probed into her mouth and she kissed him back hungrily, wanting him.

Wanting this.

When his hand travelled up beneath her dress to stroke the flesh at the top of her lacy hold-ups, she gasped. Then he kissed her neck while his hand slid up between her legs, lightly cupping her sex over the now-damp silk fabric of her knickers. She thrust back against his hand, urging him on, needing his fingers inside her.

Needing him.

Fat girls try harder.

She squeezed her eyes shut, trying to dispel the tormenting words.

Luckily distraction was at hand – Luc's fingers answered her unspoken plea, dipping beneath the elastic of her knickers to thrust up inside her sex, fondling the wetness he found there while his thumb caressed her clit. She parted her shaking legs for him, willing herself to live in the moment. Whatever this was, whatever it would turn out to be, it felt good. Even if this never lasted past tonight.

I need this.

She was so turned on already she practically jerked against him, contracting around his skilful fingers, wet and hungry for him.

"More please," she moaned softly. "I need more."

Luc's breath sounded ragged close to her ear. In response he tugged down her knickers. They lay at her feet, a scrap of turquoise silk and lace around her boots. She quickly stepped out of them, enjoying the sensation of cold air where her underwear had once been.

"Come with me." Luc released her arms and tugged her gently towards his bedroom, where he steered her down onto the bed. It felt strangely erotic to be fully clothed except for her knickers, just waiting for him to make love to her.

Pulsing with anticipation she let him push her dress up, exposing her sex to the air. Then he pulled her thighs wide apart on the edge of the bed and she rested the heels of the boots on the sheets.

"Sophie, you look so beautiful, so sexy." Luc exhaled and then knelt down between her legs, lowering his head and softly trailing a line of kisses up the inside of her thighs.

"Oh God," she moaned softly, threading her fingers into his long dark hair, aroused by the friction of the stubble gently grazing her thighs.

When his mouth finally moved to her sex, licking and teasing at her clit she arched off the bed, jolted by the sharp pleasure piercing her body. His hands caressed her bottom, squeezing and parting her buttocks, exploring her. He slid his fingers up inside her at the same time as his tongue flickered over her sensitive clit. She moaned, reaching down to thread her fingers in through his hair again.

He thrust in and out, in and out with his fingers and his tongue, watching her intently in the dim light the whole time until she tensed and throbbed in his hands, her body convulsing into orgasm, overwhelmed by waves of hot pleasure, unlike anything she'd ever experienced before.

She lay panting on the bed as he rose to his feet. The large erection evident in Luc's suit trousers was impossible to miss despite the dim light streaming through the bedroom window from a street light.

"May I?" He gestured to her dress.

She nodded, not capable of coherent speech just yet. Right now she'd let him do whatever he wanted. Anything he wanted.

Oh God, anything.

The anticipation buzzed throughout her body.

He slid the dress up over her head and then, almost reverently, stroked her breasts through the lace fabric of her bra. Her nipples stiffened even harder to his touch. She ached for him to stroke her bare breasts, to cup and kiss them. She wanted to press up against his bare chest, flesh on flesh.

She reached round and unclasped her bra, drinking in the expression on his face when her breasts bounced free from restraint.

"Mon dieu!" He stared in wonder at her breasts and for the first time Sophie felt glad of her big breasts rather than embarrassed.

He lowered a grinning mouth to one nipple and sucked hard while cupping the other breast with a hand. The soles of her feet tingled and she gasped, clasping the edge of the bed to anchor herself.

Once he had sucked each nipple in turn he lifted his head and stared at her.

"You're so beautiful, so sexy, Sophie," he repeated.

And for that brief moment she felt it, felt powerful and womanly, capable of exciting a gorgeous man like Luc.

Thomas said you were sexy. A nasty voice whispered at the back of her mind.

Fuck Thomas.

She squashed the voice back down.

Not now. All that crap wasn't going to spoil this, ruin the wonder of actually having Luc's naked body between her legs.

"Take your clothes off," she ordered, feeling powerful, carried along on the wave of his attention.

His eyes gleamed as he tore at his shirt. Unable to wait she moved off the bed to kneel in front of him, releasing his belt buckle and freeing his erection. The cotton shirt fell from Luc's hand, brushing her hair as she took him into her mouth. Her tongue tasted him, licked over the head and rolled around the length of him. When he stiffened in response she felt...powerful. Once his erection was rock hard she withdrew.

"Lie back on the bed Sophie," Luc whispered hoarsely. "Let me make love to you."

She backed down to sit on the crisp white sheet, her legs making contact with the back of the bed, her stockings and boots still on. Luc pushed her back onto the mattress, firmly pulling her thighs apart again. He paused only to grab a foil packet from the bedside table.

Even though consumed by the heady, erotic haze Sophie cursed herself. She hadn't even thought about protection.

Have you learnt nothing?

Just as well one of them was responsible.

But then all thoughts were driven from her mind as he pushed inside her, thrusting gently at first and then harder. Her head tilted back on the bed, eyes on gorgeous Luc, his dark hair wild, eyes burning into her. She opened her legs even wider, drawing her knees further up to her chest revelling in the sensation of the deeper thrusts. He snaked one hand in between them to stroke her clit as he pumped into her. Then she forgot anything at all as another orgasm ripped through her body, making her cry out as hot pleasure seared her, turned her inside out.

"Sophie." He cried out, stiffening and jerking hard inside her as she contracted around his erection.

Never had she felt this womanly, this free from inhibition.

As Luc collapsed on the bed next to her she felt the loss of him inside and tried not to let the doubts and insecurities seep back into her mind. He pulled her close, spooning behind her, warm flesh against warm flesh. Safe yet thrilling at the same time.

"Did you like that, Sophie?" He whispered in her ear, lightly stroking her breasts with his free hand.

"Oh yes."

Don't say thank you. Don't you dare.

He rolled her over onto her back and lightly tickled her collar bone, walking his fingers down between her breasts and then stroking her stomach. Something about his warm fingers caressing her skin...it felt too wonderful, too good to be true. What if he never wanted to see her after tonight?

How could she go back to not having sex after this? She'd thought she hadn't minded not having sex. Much safer to read about it in the pages of a novel. No humiliation, no disappointment.

But lonely.

And she'd never had sex like this to miss before. How could the charge between two human beings be so powerful?

"What happens next?" The question had slipped out before Sophie could stop it.

CHAPTER FOUR

With every red, heart-shaped card the barriers around her heart had been dissolving. They'd softened every time Luc said her name or smiled another sexy smile. She was hurtling head-first towards a waterfall. Could she grab at a branch before it was too late?

"What happens now is I make love to you again." Luc's hand dipped between her legs, stroking and exploring, making her sigh with pleasure. She thought she'd never get tired of his touch, never get enough of him. "Relax, Sophie."

When he lowered himself on top of her, hard thighs against her softer flesh she gasped. She never was going to grab that branch.

She'd jumped willingly into this river and let Luc sweep her away.

After producing another foil packet and sheathing himself he pressed at her entrance. She raised her legs high in the air so he could enter her more deeply, running her hands over the tight muscles of his neck and back, dipping down over his bottom, pulling him into her.

His own hands grasped the backs of her thighs, pushing them back towards the mattress as he thrust into her even deeper.

Then he maneuvered her so she was on top. She loved the sense of power as she contracted hard around him, rocking her hips back and forth. Luc's hands reached up to caress her breasts, her nipples budding against his palms as she ground down against him, feeling liberated, appreciated with every groan that left Luc's lips.

Fat girls try harder. Hell, hell, hell...will I ever forget those words?

Confidence ebbing, she slowed her movements, fear creeping into her body, paralysing her. Was she being too enthusiastic? Trying too hard?

"Sophie? Are you okay?"

She nodded her response but had to work hard to blink back the hot tears burning in her eyes.

"Stop Sophie," he ordered, raising himself up on his elbows. "Come and lie down next to me and talk to me."

This would be it, she'd share all her insecurities and he'd discreetly back off. He'd do it kindly, because he was a nice guy, but... She had to say something; it wasn't fair to leave Luc thinking it was something he'd done to upset her.

"Okay, there was this guy..." She started, burying her face in his shoulder, breathing in his comforting scent. By the time she'd finished her tale she felt a little better, lighter somehow.

Luc, on the other hand, seemed tense, clutching her hand tightly as he swore in French, both a few curses she knew and some she didn't.

"Who is he? Is he still in Verbier?" Luc's mouth was set in a grim line.

Sophie hesitated. "It doesn't matter, well okay it does but it's in the past. I need to move on. This is the first time I've...you know...since then."

Luc's eyes widened. He cupped Sophie's face in his hands. "Sophie, you're not fat, you know that, yes?"

"Well two years ago..."

"You weren't fat then, either. I only knew you from a distance then but I always thought you were gorgeous. I didn't approach you because I don't usually date seasonaires. I'm not into relationships with a short shelf life. But you were, and are, just what a woman should be – soft and womanly." His hands made curves in the air. "What man wants a hip bone jutting into him? You are gorgeous and that guy was a...what's the English word? A prick."

She stifled a giggle. "Yes, he is."

"And for me this isn't about one night only. I don't do that. I'd like us to see each other, to go out and see what happens."

"Oh." Sophie's heart lurched as though she'd suddenly stepped into a lift shaft.

He likes me too.

She couldn't stop the smile from spreading across her face. "I'd like that too."

"Come here." Luc pulled her closely against him, squeezing her so tightly her breasts were crushed against his bare chest. Maybe things could be okay?

But you haven't told him everything have you?

The whisper of doubt was back, jibing and poking at her, refusing to stay silent.

If you told him all your secrets do you think he'd still be holding you so tight?

She squeezed her eyes shut, irrationally afraid he might see the secrets lurking in her eyes. For now she refused to think about the clouds waiting to move and cover the sun. She focused only on the progress of his fingers, slowly coaxing the tension from her body. All thoughts except Luc were banished as he made love to her again, erasing the memory of Thomas from her body and her mind. Wiping her clean again.

Luc looked across at Sophie as she slept next to him. Light streamed in from outside. He'd need to wake her soon. He still felt angry when he thought about what that guy had done to her confidence.

He sighed. There wasn't much he could do about it now, other than show Sophie, prove to her that the other guy was just a jerk who knew nothing. He needed to prove to her that his interest in her wasn't just sexual. He wasn't out to use her; he knew she was afraid of that. It was pretty obvious.

He gently stroked her shoulder. "Sophie."

Her eyes opened, seemingly astonished to wake to find him next to her.

"Oh. Hi." She smiled.

"Hi." He laughed. "Did you sleep well?"

"Yes, very well." she smiled. "I couldn't work out where I was for a moment."

"Sorry to wake you up but I need to go out."

"Oh." Her smile faded. "Of course, I should probably head back to Chalet Repos. I suppose."

"Are you on breakfast duty?" he asked.

"No, but..." She frowned.

"Why don't you come with me?" He asked, gratified to see the frown vanish.

"Where are we going?" She asked once they had dressed.

"To collect my dog, Max."

"I didn't know you had a dog?" Sophie asked, surprised.

"He's a rescue. He's not great at being left alone so I took him to my parents for the night."

"How long have you had him?"

"About six months now. He seems happy to sleep in the flat when I'm working downstairs but somehow he knows the second I've left the building and starts howling."

"Why did he need rescuing?"

"Someone left him tied to a sign post. He was in a bad way, he'd had a broken leg no one had ever treated and they had to shave off most of his coat because it was so matted."

"Oh the poor thing." Sophie's eyes widened, glistening with tears. "I miss my parents' dog, Toby, while I'm in Switzerland. How does he cope with the deep snow?"

"He's got a little snow suit," Luc replied sheepishly. "Well, with his fur cut he used to shiver, I wanted to keep him warm."

"Cute." She smiled at him as they got into his jeep and he wondered if she was talking about the dog or him. "So are we going to Vex? Is that where you said your parents live?"

When they pulled up outside his parents' café Luc knew exactly what conclusions his mother would draw from him bringing Sophie along with him. But then Maman had been trying to marry him off for years.

They pushed through the thick curtain that hung across the entrance behind the door. The curtain probably preceded him; it'd been there as long as he could remember. As soon as they entered the café Max ran out from behind the bar, barking excitedly. Luc bent down to ruffle Max's ears and tried to avoid the wild volley of licks from an enthusiastic pink tongue.

"Oh, he's gorgeous." Sophie knelt down next to Max and extended a hand so he could sniff her. Max responded with a resounding lick.

"That's my boy, he has good taste." Luc grinned.

Next they were engulfed by his parents, his father complaining that Max had spent most of the night howling and they'd had to let him sleep on their bed to shut him up.

Luc smiled at the idea of his rigid 'dogs should live in kennels' father letting Max up on the bed. It was obvious his father had a soft spot for the mongrel. Luc often caught him feeding Max tidbits when he thought no one was looking.

"This is Sophie, Maman." He introduced Sophie in English, not wanting her to feel left out.

"Pleased to meet you Sophie," his mother replied in stiff, formal English, extending a hand for Sophie to shake but then changing her mind and hugging her instead, planting a kiss on both cheeks.

"It's lovely to meet you too." Sophie smiled sweetly and Luc could see his mother was instantly won over. She always made snap judgments about people.

Her judgment was usually right.

"You must join us for lunch." His mother still clasped Sophie's hand as though intending to keep her there by force, if necessary.

"I don't know, Sophie may have other plans, Maman," Luc

protested, even though he knew it was futile.

"No excuses, Luc," his mother replied firmly. "Paul and Marie are coming over with the new baby."

"Paul is my cousin," Luc explained to Sophie. He leaned in and whispered in her ear "You okay with this?"

She nodded and smiled, reaching down to stroke Max, who was desperately vying for her attention.

"Come and sit down, Sophie, Maman likes to have the kitchen to herself when she's cooking for family."

"Tsk," his mother clucked and rolled her eyes but Luc determinedly led Sophie over to a seat at one of the larger tables. This felt right. Sophie felt so unbelievably right. He shouldn't be thinking this far ahead but it was hard not to... Family was important to him and this was the first time he'd found a woman who felt like a perfect fit. It was a shame he'd only really got to know her this season.

Didn't people say when you knew, you knew?

He watched Sophie playing with Max, who'd brought her his tug-of-war toy.

He knew.

Sophie loved everything about Madame and Monsieur Dubois and the Café du Place. It was wonderfully old-fashioned with dark wood panelling and lace curtains at the windows of the old chalet. It wasn't on the main tourist trail; only a handful of old men sat at the bar nursing their drinks and a few couples sat drinking coffee.

It wasn't pretending to be something it wasn't, or charging extortionate tourist prices for a croque monsieur. Luc's mother had unapologetic grey streaks in her hair and laughter lines around her mouth.

It felt refreshing to be with "normal" people for a change, not in a place where people might judge her for her clothes or appearance. It was like a small grounding dose of being back at home in Cumbria, where straight talking was the only talking.

"So you didn't want to stay in Vex and work here with your parents?" she asked, coming back to sit down next to Luc.

"There's not enough work for me here." Luc replied, resting his hand on her thigh. She liked the warmth of his fingers through her jersey dress, remembering how they had teased her so skillfully. Heat crept up her neck.

Last night had been...incredible.

"And we would kill each other." His father called out from across the room where he was fetching a bottle of wine.

"That too." Luc grinned and Sophie laughed. Somehow she doubted it; this was a close family.

The curtain swung open and a dark-haired couple walked in with a small baby in a carry seat and one of the cutest toddlers Sophie had ever seen.

Her heart contracted.

She stayed sitting, hands clasped tightly in her lap while Luc's family converged around Luc and his parents.

You have to get over this. There are going to be lots of babies, lots of children. You can't avoid this, can't pretend it's not happening.

Even Luc coming back to sit next to her to introduce her and replacing his hand on her thigh couldn't comfort her. When the little girl, dark unruly curls tumbling down her back, swiped at Max's tail with her pudgy hands Sophie acted instinctively, sweeping Max up on her lap.

"Doucement." Sophie stroked Max's head gently to demonstrate how he should be handled, taking the little girl's hand in hers so they could gently stroke Max together.

"Elle sera une bonne maman," Luc's mother nudged him hard in the ribs, beaming.

Sophie understood.

"She will be a good mother..." Never. I can never be a mother...

She turned her face down to Max, as though stroking him were the most important thing in the world. It soothed her a little, enough to push the pain back down, to deal with another day.

When she glanced up Luc's mother was still beaming in her direction, hazel-brown eyes twinkling.

Luc rolled his eyes at Sophie. "Sorry," he mouthed.

If only you knew.

"Would you like to hold her?" Marie smiled at Sophie, extending the baby towards her.

What on earth could she say?

"Yes, thank you." She forced a smile to her lips, accepting the tiny bundle, carefully supporting the fragile skull as she brought the baby tenderly towards her chest.

Tiny black-button eyes regarded her seriously, as though to say "You might be fooling all these people but I can see everything about you Sophie."

Once in her arms she couldn't resist lifting the baby up so she could inhale that gorgeous baby smell. Instinctively she planted a kiss on the baby's head. The pain surged up inside her.

You'll never be a mother, never have a baby of your own to love and it's all your own stupid fault.

Hurriedly she passed her back to Marie before the heat burning at the back of her eyes could turn into tears she didn't want to have to explain.

Luc squeezed her thigh and despite her misery it still sent sexual electricity coursing through her body.

I still have Luc.

If only people would shut up about her making a good mother she might just be able to cope with this.

Maybe.

I may still have Luc, but for how long?

Somehow she held it together for the rest of lunch, answering the questions about her life and family in England and remembering to smile.

As soon as they were alone in Luc's jeep he turned to her. "I'm sorry about my mother, I could see she made you uncomfortable."

"Oh no, really, your mother is lovely. My mum's the same,

always on about when I'm going to give her grandchildren." Sophie turned her head away, as though looking at the view, and blinked back tears.

"It's not just that, although she does want grandchildren," Luc said. "It's kind of complicated, you see she's not really my mother."

Sophie jerked her head back towards him. "Really? But you all seem so close, closer than my family if I'm honest."

"I'm adopted. Maman couldn't have children. She always says she left it too late and how I shouldn't put business before family. Since I turned thirty she's just got worse, saying I mustn't leave it too late to settle down and become a father. They're a lot older than my friends' parents were. I didn't care about that growing up but she's always saying you should have children when you're young."

"Oh." Emotion choked Sophie and she couldn't speak but Luc stared intently at the road in front of him, lost in his own emotion, and didn't seem to notice.

"Is it just her?" Sophie faltered. "Sorry, I mean is it, you know, important to you too, or is it all about her expectations?"

"She knows I used to have a thing about not having any blood relatives when I was a child," he admitted. "Well, it never really went away but when I was older and a bit less self-centred I could see I was hurting her feelings and so I shut up about it. I think she always knew it bothered me, though."

Sophie blinked hard and couldn't speak again. It took all her effort to hold back the tsunami of emotion threatening to destroy her new fragile happiness. She turned to stare down at the Rhone Valley as they followed the twisty road down the side of the mountain.

"Sorry, Sophie, this is all really heavy." Luc reached over and gently squeezed her thigh. "Forget about it. She just assumed that we were...well it's been a while since I took a girl home. I did try to tell her we've only just started going out. Anyway, let's think about something a little more fun. Would you like to come back to my flat? You don't have to be back at Chalet Repos until tonight do you?"

Forget about it? I wish.

Yet her body fizzed with anticipation at the thought of going home with Luc, making love to him again. A surge of longing swelled inside her. So powerful she chose to be overwhelmed by it, to give in to it.

Better than thinking.

Thinking could wait.

"Yes please," she said.

"You see, you have such polite manners, no wonder my mother loves you." Luc laughed.

"She does?"

"Oh yes, she tends to make her mind up about a person in the first minutes of meeting them. Always go with your, what's the English word? Gut?"

"Yes, gut instinct," Sophie replied absently, her body aching for Luc's touch and remembering how it had felt to confide in him about Thomas. He'd been indignant on her behalf, protective and then he'd made love to her, had helped to erase the bad memories, replacing them with good ones.

Gut instinct? Right now it was telling her to grab hold of Luc and not let go.

Thinking is going to have to wait.

Once back in his apartment they settled Max on his dog bed in the living room, chewing happily on a hide bone.

"Fancy a shower?" He asked.

She nodded shyly. She'd never actually showered with a man before but the idea of getting naked with Luc under some hot, steamy water was pretty appealing. Did she fancy a shower?

Hell, yes.

Once in the bathroom they locked the door to keep Max out. Sophie took her boots off and for the second time Luc peeled off her dress. Somehow Sophie didn't feel any of her usual fear of exposing her body in daylight. Luc had made it clear he loved her body, and if he admired her breasts and soft curves maybe it was time she started to love them too.

As he swiftly took off his own clothes she unhooked her bra, revelling in the pleasure gleaming in Luc's darkening eyes.

"Parfait. Absolutely perfect." Luc pulled his jeans off and she tentatively reached out to touch his taut, warm flesh, brushing over the soft hair snaking down into the waistband of his trunks.

Leaning forward she pressed her bare breasts against his chest and slid her hands down inside his trunks, enjoying Luc's sharp intake of breath as she fondled his erection.

At some point she'd sit down and think. But not now.

Luc slid his own hands down inside her knickers, cupping her bottom and squeezing, pulling her up towards him for a kiss. As they kissed she felt her knickers pushed down to the floor. He hooked one of her legs up onto his hip and slid the stocking slowly down her leg. Then he did the same for the other leg, edging his bare thigh up between her legs, deliberately rubbing against her sex. She rubbed back, enjoying the feel of hard muscle between her legs, pressing against him, feeling sexy and wet for him and wanting him to know it.

Luc turned on the shower and pulled her under the water. The shock of cold water surprised her and she shrieked, but quickly it became warm and the water slid over and between their now-glistening bodies. She reached in between them to hold Luc's stiffening erection, caressing the length of it, her other hand reaching round to explore his tight bottom, hardly able to believe she got to do this.

For real. Not just read about it in a novel.

He groaned as she squeezed his erection. Then he lifted her up so she was perched on the chrome rail. The cold surface against her bare bottom made her gasp. He closed in, holding a foil wrapper in one hand. Once he'd sheathed himself she wrapped her legs around him, her heels pressing into his bottom.

He thrust into her and she arched her back, pushing against

him so he entered her even deeper. Her breasts jutted towards him, warm water cascading from them.

She felt so sexy, so powerful.

Sex had never felt like this before.

With both hands she held herself steady on the bar while she bucked against him, meeting his rhythm. They never broke eye contact and as she stared into Luc's eyes she felt it: a connection, something extraordinary. It pierced her with joy and washed away the loneliness she'd secretly carried for years. She wanted this. She needed this.

She'd waited forever for Luc.

You have to tell him.

Of all the times...The voice was back, insistent, persistent even when Luc lowered his mouth to her breast and lightly nipped her nipple. She spasmed, driving him even deeper inside her. She thrust back hard, as though she might drive the voice away.

She couldn't tell him, not now. They'd only just begun, which meant they weren't due any heavy conversations for ages, surely.

Except he raised the issue himself today.

But what if this was just a fling for Luc? Why put herself through a horrible conversation if there was no need?

This isn't a fling; it's something more. He said he doesn't do casual relationships.

The way Luc was looking at her she knew he felt it too – this intimacy, this tipping past the point of no return.

But I've waited so long for this.

She blocked out the voice as Luc reached in between them to stroke slow circles on her clit as he thrust into her. After only a few strokes Sophie cried out, jerking and spasming as she came. Her skin tingled all the way down to her toes as he held her tightly, clasping her to his chest so she didn't slip. Then he came too, jerking inside her so violently she had to hold onto the rail to stop them both falling to the floor.

"Sophie" he called out, half groan, half sigh.

He was perfect for her, so perfect.

It's not fair.

She didn't need to tell him, of course she didn't. But wouldn't it then be a ticking bomb for the next six months...a year? How could she live with that? Falling even harder for Luc, knowing there was an expiry date on the relationship.

Because Luc would dump her. It was just a question of when.

CHAPTER FIVE

When Sophie walked back into Chalet Repos it was fairly quiet. Most of the guests would still be on the piste. Happy toddler chatter came from the living room, the older children must still be out with their parents.

Sophie walked into the room to find Holly sitting on her heels on a cow-hide rug on the floor, building a Lego tower with three-year-old Lettie. Lettie seemed to be dominating the one-sided conversation, acting as architect, engineer and foreman for the construction, her blonde bunches bouncing up and down as she surveyed her project. Holly was clearly a handy, adult-sized labourer.

"Babysitting?" Sophie almost managed a smile as she flopped down onto a dark leather sofa but it was too much effort. Could she really talk to Holly about this?

I have to talk to someone.

"Phi," Lettie squealed, turning at the sound of Sophie's voice. She'd only been able to master the second syllable of Sophie's name since her family had been staying at Chalet Repos. Her pure, unadulterated joy at seeing Sophie made something twist painfully in Sophie's chest. It both hurt and made her happy at the same time.

Yet now Sophie did manage a smile, accepting the proffered piece of Lego.

"I'm just babysitting for the afternoon," Holly replied, turning to scrutinise her, a small smirk playing at the corner of her mouth. "Never mind me, how about you?! Good date? Did the dress do the trick?"

"You could say that." Sophie smiled sheepishly, smoothing the dress hem down onto her knees. Returning home in the same clothes you left in the previous evening was a bit of a giveaway.

"How was the W?" Holly asked. "I've heard it's amazing, I'm dropping hints for Scott to take me there for my birthday."

"It's amazing." Sophie rested back against the cushions, glad to have an easy question to answer. "Really trendy, but stylish and it's staffed by The Beautiful People, seriously Holly, they must have recruited from a model agency. And they're all really nice too, not like the staff at some trendy restaurants who look down their noses at you. And the cocktails, you have to have one of the cocktails..."

"I'm working on it; you've given me some good ammunition to use against Scott." Holly grinned. "So you had a good evening then? And you like Luc?"

"Luc's lovely," Sophie said, sighing.

"Phi." Lettie reached her arms up, asking for a cuddle, bored with the adult conversation. Heart twisting again, Sophie picked her up, inhaling the scent of her strawberry shampoo. Someone was really trying to rub it in today.

Rub it in or force you to talk about it? Maybe it will get worse and worse until I actually deal with it?

As Lettie put small pudgy arms around Sophie's neck Sophie couldn't stop the hot tears escaping, rolling silently down her cheeks.

All my fault.

"Sophie, what's wrong, lovely?" Holly got up from the floor and came to sit down next to Sophie on the sofa, taking Lettie from her. "Would you like a DVD Lettie? How about your Barbie DVD?"

Once the DVD was on and Lettie had been placed cross-legged on a cushion, sucking her thumb, Holly came back to the sofa.

"So," Holly sat down and handed Sophie a clean tissue from her pocket. "Do you want to talk about it?"

Sophie gratefully accepted the tissue and blotted away the tears from her cheeks. If only she could blot away her dilemma. But keeping it quiet and buried just wasn't working for her anymore. Denial had its faults as a problem-solving policy.

"Yes," Sophie replied and registered the flicker of surprise in Holly's eyes. Understandable that given her standard response was 'I'm fine' when anyone asked if she was okay.

Holly sat quietly, pulling her long auburn hair up into a ponytail, waiting for Sophie to speak. Lettie sat equally quietly, entranced by the television, all interest in Lego and 'Phi' temporarily forgotten.

"I can't have children, Holly," Sophie said, staring down at the sodden tissue in her hands as she twisted and shredded it.

"Tash did say...something," Holly said quietly.

"Bloody Tash." Sophie's hands clenched around the tissue and she frowned.

"She said we had to shut up about you being so good with kids, that it was upsetting you." Holly smiled sympathetically. "If it makes it any better she only told me and Amelia, Lucy already knew."

"Oh, I see." Sophie's indignation seeped away and her shoulders sagged. Had she actually told Tash not to tell anyone? Sophie automatically kept any confidence, but experience had taught her you needed to be specific with Tash.

She unclenched her fists. It had been thoughtful of Tash to say what she had. She was, despite everything, a good friend. She stared out towards the view, trying to gather the courage to tell Holly the full story. The late-afternoon sun slanted into the room, bathing the wooden floorboards with light.

"Isn't it a bit early to be worrying about how that might affect Luc?" Holly asked gently.

"And leave it as a ticking time bomb? When should I tell him?" Sophie turned to face Holly, hot tears streaming steadily down her cheeks again. "When I've had time to really fall in love with him? To get used to having him in my life, only to lose him? I think it's probably better to end it now."

Saying the words made it suddenly real, unbearably real.

This just isn't fair. I've waited so long for someone special...

"Are you sure it would be a deal-breaker for him?" Holly asked, frowning. "Some guys don't want kids; it might even be a plus. I mean in their eyes, obviously. I understand it's a huge thing for you, of course it is."

"He isn't one of them," Sophie said miserably. "I know, he kind of told me how important having his own family was. It's a major priority for him."

"He told you that on the first date?" Holly raised her eyebrows.

"It was his mother who said something, said I'd make a good mother, can you believe it?" Sophie half-laughed, half-sobbed.

"He introduced you to his parents already?" Holly asked, eyebrows arching even higher.

"It wasn't like that." Sophie shook her head. "We went over to collect his dog and they insisted we stay for lunch. He saw what his mother said had made me uncomfortable and it all came out about him being adopted. He wants blood relatives and I'll never be able to give them to him. So you see, I should walk away, it's only fair to him."

Sophie sobbed, lowering her face into her hands, the pent-up sadness of the past two years welling up towards the breach in the dam.

It's all my fault.

"What about what's fair for you, Sophie? You're so great at putting everyone else first, but what about your needs?" Holly put one hand on Sophie's arm while the other stroked her back. "In all the years I've known you you've never been like this over a man. He's obviously special to you. Special full stop, in fact. How many men would go to the bother of setting up a treasure hunt?"

"I know," Sophie's voice cracked and she tried to pull herself together. "It doesn't feel fair, but then life isn't, is it? Anyway, there's more, there's the reason why I can't have kids."

Sophie looked back down at her hands, at the mangled tissue. Holly gently took her hands and squeezed them, not seeming to care about the tissue. Sophie forced herself to take a deep breath, summoning all her courage.

"Do you remember Thomas?" A sense of relief flooded her now she'd made the decision to confide in someone. She wasn't sure she had other options open to her. Now the dam holding back her emotions had cracked she didn't think she'd be able to stop the secrets from leaking out.

"I think so." Holly continued to stroke Sophie's back. "Was he the guy who did really well in the Verbier High Five and turned pro?"

"Huh. Yes, you probably would remember that detail. He went on about it rather a lot," Sophie replied grimly. "Well, we slept together but he didn't use protection. I asked him to but he just ignored me, carried on, you know... I should've stopped him, should've insisted but... Well, I was on the pill anyway and I really fancied him. I was flattered. I didn't want to be difficult. Stupid huh?"

Holly gave Sophie's hands another squeeze.

Sophie sighed. "Plus we'd had a few cocktails, but if I'm honest I can't blame the alcohol. I was sober enough to have insisted and I should've done."

They lapsed into silence. For a moment the Barbie DVD was the only sound in the room. The light outside changed from gold to pink and red as the sun set behind the mountains.

"What happened?" Holly prompted Sophie gently.

"I caught something from him...an...an infection, and it developed into pelvic inflammatory disease. My ovaries are now so badly scarred that I...I can't... It would be impossible for me to ever..." Sophie couldn't finish the sentence, it hurt too much. She barely recognised her own voice. It sounded like a stranger relating her secrets, not her.

Yet now she'd told someone she did feel better, a little lighter. As though some of the leaden misery she'd been carrying around had been released into the atmosphere, its power diminished.

"Oh Soph, I'm so sorry." Holly edged closer, pulling Sophie towards her and holding her tight.

Sophie let herself lean into the hug, let the comfort soothe her a little. Until she thought about Luc, about the connection she was turning her back on and then she couldn't stop the sob that rose up from her chest.

Lettie got up from her cushion and walked over, picking up a Lego man to offer Sophie.

Sophie smiled at Lettie through her tears. "Thank you, sweetie. I'm okay, don't worry. Go back and watch your DVD."

Lettie made her way back to her cushion and lay on her stomach, propping herself up on her elbows, eyes fixed back on the screen.

Holly glanced over to check, Lettie wasn't listening. "Are you sure there's no chance?"

"Yes." Sophie sighed again. "One in five PID sufferers become infertile and guess what? I was unlucky."

"Very unlucky." Holly grimaced.

"But really it was my fault." Sophie bit her lip.

"How?" Holly asked indignantly. "No one could judge you for this. If it's anyone's fault it's Thomas's."

"Thanks but I share the blame too," Sophie insisted. It was kind of Holly to make her feel better, but she'd had a choice that night.

"You made a mistake, that's all." Holly said, squeezing Sophie's shoulders. "Everyone makes mistakes, it's just that most of the time we get away with them. Lots of us have got caught up in the moment, Sophie, it really doesn't make you a bad person. You're not the first one to have sex without a condom and you won't be the last."

Sophie looked gratefully at Holly. "So, what should I do? I really, really like Luc, I think I might've even fallen in love with him. Does that sound crazy?"

"Not crazy, no." Holly smiled. "One minute you're floating above cloud nine and the next you're down to earth with a bump and a nice side-helping of despair. People who've never fallen in love just think you're crazy or are developing bipolar disorder. I've been there, but these things have a habit of working out. If I were you I'd leave it for a while. Get to know each other and wait for the right time to tell him."

"Maybe." Sophie sniffed, dabbing away the last of her tears. If she left it longer perhaps he'd become more attached to her, fall in love with her too and be willing to choose her over the chance to have his own children?

That's not fair to Luc. You know what you have to do Sophie.

Yes, she knew and it sucked.

"Hi there." Luc smiled when Sophie walked into Café des Amis. Then he noticed her eyes were red-rimmed and her returning smile seemed a little strained. He put down the glasses he was holding. "Are you okay?"

She half inclined her head as though about to nod but then abandoned the gesture. "Can we talk Luc? Are you able to leave the bar?"

"Yes, Stefan can cope for twenty minutes. Let's go upstairs. Max will be happy to see you." Luc wondered what had happened to upset Sophie. Protectiveness stirred within him; he wanted to make her happy and keep her happy and would do anything in his power to make that happen.

Max came hurtling down the corridor the second Luc put his key in the lock. He leapt up first at Luc and then at Sophie. Sophie bent down to scratch Max behind the ears but she smiled tightly, as though someone had turned down the dimmer switch on her mood.

Luc put his arm around Sophie, pulling her towards him, needing to know what had happened. "Tell me what's upsetting you, please."

She turned her face to look up at him and he was surprised at the depth of pain in her eyes. He tightened his hold instinctively, wanting her to lean on him, to trust him...

"I know we've only just started, you know, seeing each other." She turned her face back down to the floor, cheeks flushed, watching Max who was jumping up at them, wanting their attention. "But there's something I need to tell you. It might change your mind about me and I'd rather get it over with now, before we...you know..."

He couldn't imagine anything that would put him off Sophie. She was sexy, kind, loyal and loving... Even his mother approved of her, which had to be a first.

She was perfect.

Perfect for him, anyway.

"Go on," he said gently. "But I really can't imagine..."

She cut him off, interrupting. "Most couples don't have this conversation this early, I know; but because of what you said I have to tell you... I can't have children, Luc, I'm infertile so...so... there could never be anything long-term between us. Not that I'm assuming you want anything long-term, but... Well, I can't start something if I know it's already got an expiry date stamped on it."

She spoke so quickly it was hard to take what she was saying in, to process it. He blinked hard, staring into space, his mind whirling.

"You were right to tell me, Sophie," he spoke slowly, as though hoping the right words would come to him if he waited long enough.

I need to be a father. I need my own family.

Could he really put all that aside for Sophie? It was a big ask. A huge decision that he couldn't make in just a few minutes. He hesitated while she stayed silent, as though waiting for more from him.

"I need to think," he said softly, trying to speak kindly. He hated the flash of pain in her eyes. The last thing he wanted was to hurt her.

What we have is special.

But he had to be honest. He couldn't lie about something as important as this. Sophie didn't reply, just stared hard down at Max, stroking his head as though it were the most important thing in the world to do right now. Pity and sympathy for her overwhelmed him.

It must have been so hard for her to tell me.

"Do you understand?" He asked gently. "I'm not saying anything. It's just it's a big decision, I need to..."

"You need to think, I know. That's only fair." Sophie looked up at him then, staring at him intently, as though committing his face to memory. "I need to go back to Chalet Repos. I've got the dinner dishes to clear up."

"Sophie," he protested, sighing. He didn't know what to say to fix this. He didn't want to hurt her but he couldn't lie, couldn't pretend it wasn't going to matter to him down the line.

I just need time to think...

"It's okay," Sophie smiled but her eyes glittered with unshed tears and he felt like a bastard.

I can't bear this.

Sophie barely saw the flight of stairs on her way down or the customers in Bar des Amis. Her eyes blurred with tears and her chest felt tight, like she couldn't breathe because something was clutching her lungs and heart and squeezing them tightly. She pulled her phone out of her pocket on the way back to Chalet Repos.

I have to end it before I can change my mind. I have to do the right thing. He's a nice guy, he doesn't want to hurt my feelings, but...

That moment of indecision in Luc's eyes when she'd told him the news had felt like a blade slicing into her heart, making it bleed. The indecision had told her everything she needed to know.

No more.

She couldn't stretch this out, prolong it. There was no point. This wasn't going to end happily. He wanted kids; she couldn't have them. He might carry on dating her out of sympathy and they could probably both do a good job of ignoring the facts for a while. But they couldn't ignore them forever and it would split them up in the end. So there was only one answer.

She had to end it now.

If it hurts this much to walk away from him now, just think how bad it would be down the line.

She put the phone back into her pocket so she could rub her cold hands together. She'd been in such a hurry to come and see Luc she'd slipped her coat on and not bothered with gloves or a hat and now her hands felt numb.

When she'd managed to get some feeling back into her fingers she retrieved the phone and typed a text message.

'Luc, thanks so much for everything. We both know it's best to call it quits. Thanks again. S x'

She pressed send before she could reconsider and then switched her phone off so she couldn't be persuaded out of the decision. If he tried to persuade her, that was. And if he didn't attempt to change her mind she'd be upset he hadn't tried. Best to leave it switched off.

So, that was that. A lovely dream over.

Back to reality.

Luc paced the flat, Max trotting at his heels, frustrated by the engaged tone he got every time he tried to ring Sophie's phone. She'd ignored the texts he'd sent in reply to hers.

It had barely been a few minutes after she'd left that he'd got her message.

'We both know it's best to call it quits.'

He didn't know anything of the sort. All he'd asked for was time to think about her news. He hadn't wanted for things to end between them.

This isn't right. I can't lose Sophie. She's special.

When his phone rang he answered it immediately without checking, the caller display.

"Luc." His mother's voice greeted him and Luc felt disappointment, swiftly followed by unease. Maman never rang his mobile when he was working.

"What's wrong?" he asked, feeling every muscle in his body tense.

When they'd finished talking he grabbed his car keys. He had to get to the hospital in Sion.

A heart attack.

He felt stiff with shock as he gave instructions to Stefan regarding locking up. Papa had always seemed indestructible. This was a wake-up call. His parents were already considerably older than his friends' parents. One day he was going to lose them. Of course he always knew that, in theory. But this made it actually seem real.

He climbed into the driver's seat of the jeep, jaw tensed. Getting hold of Sophie would have to wait. He drove too fast down to the Rhone Valley and along the autoroute to Sion, as though his presence would make his father be okay. After a frustratingly long time he managed to park in the crowded hospital car park and locate the waiting room. He spotted his mother before she saw him. She sat with her spine ramrod straight, her hair and clothes neat. But on closer inspection he noticed her eyes were bloodshot and she was still wearing her slippers.

It was the slippers that got to him. They made her look vulnerable, somehow. He swallowed down his emotion; she needed him to be strong. He sat down next to her, feeling out of his depth. How could he comfort her?

Yet when she turned to greet him she seemed far more composed than him. All his certainties were shifting and he felt adrift. He usually felt like he could deal with anything. But this...

"I like that girl Sophie," she said, once they'd established there was no news yet; Papa was still in surgery.

Luc guessed she was trying to distract herself while they waited for the prognosis. Best to humour her.

"She's lovely. Perfect," he said guardedly.

"So, marry her," she said, fixing her dark-brown eyes on him.

"Maman! It's too early to talk about marriage," he exclaimed. Why were they having this discussion now, while Papa was in surgery? He lowered his voice, "And there's a problem, she can't have children."

"Poor girl," she clucked and sucked in her breath, frowning. "I wouldn't wish that on anyone. But Luc, think about what happened to me. If I'd been able to have my own babies we never would have given you a home."

He stared uncertainly at her and she laid her hand on top of his, her fingers tightening their hold, an acknowledgement they were in dangerous territory.

Luc didn't answer, his throat felt tight, his eyes suspiciously watery.

"You never asked about your birth mother. Did you ever search for her?'" Her sudden question took him aback. It seemed Papa's heart attack had broken through the usual barriers they'd put around the subject by mutual consent, taking them out of dangerous territory and onwards into uncharted lands.

Luc stared at his mother, wondering where all this was coming from. Maybe she, like Luc, had been jolted by a sense of her own mortality and wanted to make sure the important things were said.

He shook his head.

"Why not?" she asked.

"I didn't want to know. You're my mother," he said.

I didn't want to hurt your feelings. But also, why would I want to know the woman who didn't want me?

"Your birth mother was an addict in Geneva. She neglected you and you were taken away from her. Your father is unknown, possibly one of her clients." Her words were like bullets, delivered calmly and almost dispassionately.

He flinched from her.

"You wonder why I'm saying this? Why I'm hurting you?" she asked, her voice softening and bloodshot hazel eyes regarding him kindly.

"You're upset about Papa," Luc said uncertainly, still trying to process what she'd said about his birth mother. This evening was swiftly turning into one of the worst of his life. First Sophie, then the phone call and then this...

"Because I don't want you to make a mistake you might regret forever. You need to know real family isn't blood, it's the choice, the decision to love." She raised her hands to cup his jaw, forcing her to look at him. "Blood isn't everything. Maybe I should've told you the truth years ago. Don't make a mistake you'll regret, Luc, we don't get that much time."

She gestured around the waiting room, a crack in her voice, a tear leaking out of the corner of her eye. He squeezed her hands, understanding her. Loving her. Wishing he could protect her from this. Like he'd wished he could protect Sophie.

He sighed heavily. "I know, Maman, I don't want to lose her. She is special. But, I don't know, I'm confused."

"At least we're agreed on one thing – Sophie is special, so think about your options. If you marry..." She waved his attempt to interrupt away. "I know you say it's too soon but I knew I'd marry your father within an hour of meeting him, it was a coup de foudre."

Love at first sight.

Her eyes misted up and he reached for the box of tissues resting on the waiting-room table alongside ancient magazines. He didn't want to think about why they'd been placed there. His stomach lurched as he thought about his father in surgery and the moment a doctor would open the waiting room door to give them news.

"Our time on this earth is short, Luc, don't waste it, and don't throw something special away."

He snorted.

"Just make sure you hold on to what's important, Luc," she replied primly. "I don't want you to have regrets."

Luc sat, his thoughts wrestling for clarity amidst the confusion, unable to answer as his eyes fixed on a pamphlet about diabetes on the opposite wall. His mother had never spoken to him like this before. The truth about his birth parents had jolted him, almost as badly as the news about Papa's heart attack. And then, of course, Sophie's news.

Trouble comes in threes.

Deep down he'd always feared the truth about his birth parents would be unpalatable; it had been an additional reason not to go looking.

He stared at the door, watching, waiting for more news, at a total loss to know what to say. Surely he'd had all the bad news he deserved for one night? The surgery had to work, it had to.

When the door finally opened, both he and his mother started. Now it was his mother's turn to be unable to speak, so he had to take charge, asking all the right questions until the message sunk in.

The surgery had been successful.

"Thank God," he whispered, feeling as though he'd aged ten years in one day. Emotion welled up inside him and suddenly he wished Sophie was here at his side.

As they rose to go to the cafeteria to wait for Papa to be taken out of recovery and brought down to a ward there was only one thought in his mind.

Sophie.

CHAPTER SIX

Sophie, Tash and Lucy relaxed on the cantine deck chairs, soaking up the sun, their skis in the rack. This would be Sophie's last season in Verbier; she couldn't do this anymore, couldn't bear to be on Luc's doorstep and permanently reminded of what she couldn't have.

Maybe Italy next year? Or France?

There were lots of different resorts where she could find work. She sighed, squeezing her eyes shut, trying to hold the pain back.

"Excusez-moi mademoiselle."

She opened her eyes to see Stefan from Bar des Amis standing in front of her with Max on a lead. Max wore his all-in-one snow suit and in his mouth was a waterproof package.

Her heart contracted.

"Hi Max." She stroked the dog's head, then looked up at Stephan. "Pour moi?"

He nodded and grinned.

She took the package from Max and made a fuss of him, receiving several licks in response.

Stefan waved goodbye and set off with Max in tow. Hands trembling, she opened the package and drew out a red, heart-shaped card. She stared at it for a while before turning it over. It had been three days since she'd texted Luc. She hadn't been able to bring herself to read his texts. Nor had she been able to delete them.

I set you a hunt,
But the treasure was you.
I can't lose what we've started,
Will you follow this clue?

Come tonight to where friends meet,
Come at eleven and we'll sit and eat.
Let me talk, persuade you to stay,
I promise, you and me, somehow we'll find a way.

Sophie put a hand to her mouth, stifling a sob. Relief and emotion mingling to send adrenalin coursing through her body. Could he really mean this? She stood up and made her way to walk past the others. She needed to get her skis, go back to Chalet Repos. She needed to think about what this could mean.

"Hey, don't leave us in suspense." Tash grabbed her arm. "Is everything okay? What does it say?"

Sophie hesitated then handed it over, unable to stop beaming and perfectly willing to share her happiness. Tash and Lucy both scrutinised the card, heads together, one dark and one blonde with pink stripes. Once read they looked up from the card, both grinning.

"So, he's going to cook for you once the bar's closed? Top bloke. You need to hold onto this one, Sophie," Tash said.

"Yes, I think you're right," Sophie replied, smiling, although a part of her struggled against it.

Nothing is solved, how can it be? You ought to walk away.

Sod that! No way could she ignore this invitation. She positively refused to, desperately wanting to see him again. She longed to feel his arms around her, leaving her breathless with need, then satisfying that need over and over.

'We'll find a way.' Does he really mean that?

She'd had a long time to try to come to terms with the effects of PID. Months to come to the conclusion that it was all very well having plans about how you expected your life to turn out – the job, the home, the husband and kids... Stuff happened. You had to adapt and survive, re-evaluate what was really important.

Maybe Luc had taken some time to think, to make changes to his own travel itinerary. If he was willing to do that for her then she most definitely would hold onto him.

It's not fair to ask him...

She frowned at the niggling thought as she snapped into her skis.

But I haven't asked him to do anything. This is his choice, his decision...

Having to take a different path to the one you'd planned was only a disaster if you let it be. Anyway, what was the alternative? Sitting around feeling sorry for yourself?

No thank you.

The Bar des Amis was quiet and the lights down so low, at first Sophie thought it was closed and Luc not, at home. Tentatively she knocked on the wooden frame of the locked door, peering through the glass to see candles flickering on all the window sills and along the bar.

Luc opened it and stepped back to let her in.

"Are you expecting a power cut?" she asked, hoping to break the tension. Her heart pounded hard against her rib cage, as though trying to break out, and she had to clasp her hands together to stop them trembling. Just being close to him again felt overwhelming. "Sorry, it looks lovely, I was just trying to..."

"I know." Luc stepped towards her, jaw peppered with stubble, eyes dark. There were dark circles beneath his eyes, as though he'd had little or no sleep. She could sympathise with that but at least she'd managed to hide the evidence with concealer.

He was wearing Diesel jeans and a dark, long-sleeved T-Shirt so she was glad she'd opted for smart casual: a pretty beaded top with her best jeans.

A table was set behind him, decorated with gold and silver stars and flickering tea lights.

He's done this for me.

Warmth spread through her body.

"Come here," Luc ordered and Sophie stepped into his arms, sighing deeply as they closed around her.

Like coming home.

Yet even while inhaling his delicious masculine scent Sophie couldn't quash the voice of doubt, despite having given it a stern talking to before leaving Chalet Repos.

Nothing has changed.

She ignored it, there was nothing on earth that could make her pull out of Luc's arms right now. But she turned her face up towards him, needing to know.

"Are you sure?" she asked, looking up at him, fear flickering inside her, despite all her best intentions and advice she knew to be sound from Holly and the girls. "You know, about what I said?"

Shut up, Sophie, don't ruin this.

"I'm sure, you're special Sophie," he said firmly. "You'll make a good mother to someone one day, I've no doubt of it. My own mother did, even though she was never able to actually give birth. You already are a good mother to all the new chalet girls each season. I've seen you watching out for them."

She bit her lip. "So you really wouldn't mind? If we ended up together, I mean?"

"Ssh." He placed a finger on her lip, where she'd bitten it. "I needed time to think; I've thought and I know I'd consider myself very lucky indeed to have you in my life."

Then he kissed her, his warm lips and tongue tasting of brandy. She melted into the kiss, tensions and fear ebbing away, finally feeling a kind of peace for the first time in ages. Had the storm really passed over, could she believe it? If they could weather this storm she was sure they'd survive others too.

Max came hurtling down into the bar, barking and jumping up at them, wanting to be included in whatever was going on.

"How did you get out?" Luc laughed. "He must have jumped the stair gate I put up. He's a creature of habit; he's used to having my company once the bar is closed. If I break the normal routine he finds a way to tell me I'm doing it wrong."

Sophie reached down and fondled Max's ears. "Poor thing, he just wants some attention. Dogs are pack animals, they need company."

And so do I.

"Would you like to be in our pack, Sophie?" Luc asked, squeezing her waist. One hand travelled over the small of her back, making warm need burn between her legs.

"Yes please." She rested her head against his chest, enjoying the sensation of strong arms around her, appreciating her body.

Arms belonging to a man she could actually trust.

"What do you say we put Max on his bed in the living room and spend some time, um, making up for lost time?" Luc's eyes gleamed and his hand pressed hard against the small of her back, fingers splaying out over her bottom, sending a sparks of pleasure vibrating through her body.

"That sounds good to me," she replied, pressing herself hard against his body, gratified to feel his hard erection. "What do you plan to do to me?"

"Wait and see," he smiled.

"Thank you," she whispered, resting her cheek against his chest for a moment.

"What for?"

"For being my Secret Valentine, for doing all this, and for what you're about to do to me." Then she looped her arms up around his neck and kissed him, hoping this meant she'd never need dread another Valentine's Day again. Eyes darkening, he led her up the stairs to his flat.

Going to bed with a book was good and she'd always love

reading, but going to bed with Luc was infinitely preferable. A real Luc over an imaginary Nathan? No contest.

Even if he did turn out to hog the duvet.

EPILOGUE

Holly walked into the living room of Chalet Repos with a tray laden with mugs of frothy hot chocolate. She was pleased Sophie had come to see them. She'd really missed her this season. She'd got used to some of the other girls coming and going and some of them she'd even stayed friends with. But Sophie had been here from the start. She'd even been at Chalet Repos before Holly had! That was an odd thought.

So she really cared about her. And that was going to make it hard to keep her mouth shut today about both her own news and also what she knew would be happening tonight.

"So, what's the plan then, Sophie?" Tash asked, perched on the arm of the sofa, taking a mug of hot chocolate from the tray.

"You deliver the first clue directly to Luc. Lucy is taking the other clues to their locations." Sophie grinned, sitting down on the squishy leather sofa, signaling to Max to sit down on the floor next to her. Then she turned to Holly. "Given he did a Valentine's treasure hunt for me last year, I thought it was only fair I should do one for him this year."

It felt strange seeing Sophie here at Chalet Repos now she no longer worked here, like old times. Holly smiled at Sophie and lowered the tray so she could take a mug.

"Yes, Tash told me. I think it's a lovely idea. So, how's it going working with Luc at the bar?" Holly sat down. She grabbed every chance she could to sit down nowadays, she hadn't expected to feel this tired.

Should I tell Sophie?

But Sophie seemed so happy at the moment it would be cruel to unsettle her, especially today.

You're going to have to tell her sometime.

"It's going great," Sophie beamed, fishing a dog treat out of her pocket for Max, now sitting at her feet, looking up mournfully at the plate of biscuits. "Not for dogs, Max."

"How is Luc's dad now?" Lucy asked, tucking her petite legs up underneath her on the armchair.

"He's doing okay. Luc goes over there to see them now and then but it's a battle to get them to accept any help." Sophie said. "And what about you Holly, any news?"

She raised an eyebrow and looked down meaningfully at Holly's stomach.

Oh crap, she's guessed. Or someone has told her.

She'd thought she disguised the bump well today with a long tunic top and leggings. After all she was only three months' gone.

"You told her?" Holly stared accusingly at Tash.

Tash held her hands up, palms facing Holly, a flash of irritation in her cat-like eyes. "It wasn't me."

"No one told me, I guessed." Sophie said. "Congratulations. It's okay, you don't need to protect me. I'm pleased for you, really I am."

"Really? I was so worried, I didn't know how to tell you." Holly sat down next to Sophie on the sofa. "It's not going to be weird if I talk to you about it?"

"No, it's not going to be weird, we won't let it be. I can still be happy for you," Sophie said quietly. "I'd be a pretty miserable cow if I wanted everyone else to suffer too. And I'm in a different place now I've had time to think more about it. It's always going to be something...very sad but it doesn't hurt quite as much as it used to. And Luc's made me see I could still be a mother to kids who really need a family."

"You're going to adopt?" Holly asked, thinking how lucky the kids would be who ended up with Sophie and Luc as their parents. "Ooh, our children could have play dates together."

Sophie smiled. "Not quite yet, but soon I think. It might depend on what happens after today, you know, the finale of the Valentine's treasure hunt. Now are you sure you're okay to deliver the first clue Tash? You're not tied up doing the Valentine's ski dating this year?"

"No." Tash shrugged, her features hardening and her usually expressive eyes inscrutable.

Hmm, interesting.

Tash was a...challenging employee at the best of times but Tash in a black mood needed careful handling. Holly felt for the girl, she sensed she'd had a bad time at home, she never talked about her family and Holly could sympathise with that.

This seemed more than a usual bad mood, though. Once today was over she'd have to find out. Being single on Valentine's Day wasn't much fun, maybe whatever was bugging her would blow over.

"So, at the end of the treasure hunt you're actually going to ask him to marry you?" Lucy asked. "That's so romantic."

"That's the plan." Sophie grinned. "And if he says yes, I'll be Sophie Dubois instead of plain old Trent. It sounds much more exotic, don't you think?"

"Good for you," Lucy said, beaming.

"I'm just a bit nervous," Sophie admitted shyly, reaching down to dispense another dog treat to Max. "I mean, what if he says no?"

"I've got a feeling he's going to say yes." Holly sipped at her hot chocolate to conceal the twitching, secret smile she knew was on her lips.

It was so hard to keep her mouth shut but it would be mean of her to spoil the surprise for Sophie, best she found out from Luc.

Once Sophie had left with Max, Holly turned to Tash, grinning. She caught sight of herself in the mirror; she looked like the Cheshire Cat. These damn hormones were making her feel so emotional.

"What's the secret then?" Tash asked, eyes regarding her shrewdly. "I can tell you know something. Is Luc planning something for Sophie again this year?"

"Yes," Holly grinned. "But the best bit is he's going to ask her to marry him tonight too."

"Oh," Tash's eyes widened. "So, how will that work out?"

"Luckily they both had the idea of ending up at the W again. They're both such romantics, wanting to go back to where they had their first date." She smiled. "Also I phoned the W to update them, just so they know only one table is needed. And as for it all coming together, well these things have a habit of working out. They'll both be there. If necessary I'll deliver them to the W myself."

"I wonder who will ask the question first." Tash crossed the room and stared out at the view but not before Holly had glimpsed the sadness in her eyes.

Tomorrow she'd sit down and have a talk with Tash, see if there was anything she could do to help. Maybe she was missing Sophie.

But for now Holly had her own Valentine's Day dinner with Scott to prepare for. Not to mention two treasure hunts to keep an eye on to make sure nothing went wrong with Luc's and Sophie's day. There was one thing she was sure of – romance wasn't dead.

And this Valentine's Day was going to be one to remember.

www.ingramcontent.com/pod-product-compliance
Lightning Source LLC
Chambersburg PA
CBHW010644100726
47900CB00011B/2970